FOREVER LOVE'N COWBOY

Billionaire Cowboys of Lone Star, Texas,
Book Six

DEBRA CLOPTON
Writing as International Bestselling Author
HOPE MOORE

Forever Love'n Cowboy

The romance that started it all… when the Buckley brothers tried to fix up their brother Tucker's friend Jace—they didn't know they were next!

Eight years ago, just before they were to be married, Lila Willis walked away, believing a lie about Jace Calhoun, and she never came back to Lone Star, Texas, to visit her gram *or* to chance a glimpse at the man who'd broken her heart.

Rancher Jace Calhoun had lost the love of his life because she'd believed the worst of him and left without hearing him out. She had driven out of town and he hadn't gone after her to try to change her mind. After all, *how could he love someone who believed he was that low?*

That's how it all began but now, after years of staying away, Lila is back in town to help her injured grandmother, who owns the store next to Jace's grandfather's feed store—the place their romance began. And of course, Jace's large dog, a Weimaraner—or *"Weim"*—loves to love on people, and makes sure Jace and Lila meet again, right from the start.

Jace's life changed years earlier when the woman he loved left. Now she's back, so what's he going to do about it?

Enjoy this introduction to Lone Star, Texas, and the Buckley family and all their friends—you're going to love these cowboys as they find their happily-ever-afters in this small Texas town full of love, laughter, and promises of forever.

CHAPTER ONE

Lila Willis pulled her topless red Jeep onto Main Street of Lone Star, Texas, the tiny town she spent summers in with her grandmother, Josie Jane Willis. It had always been a fun time in her life. There hadn't been much there other than a huge feed store—which she wasn't going to think about right now. Then there was the Mulberry Diner, which she still remembered for its wonderful breakfast and lunches. As she drove down the street, she saw many more secondhand stores and antiques stores than before, and she also spotted a hair salon and a new clothing store. Basically, it was still the same, just a few more stores—which was good because it showed the small town was still trudging along. Her grandmother owned one of those secondhand stores, called Josie Jane's Wash and Repeat and loved filling it with *"things that needed a second chance or a fresh start"* as Gram loved to say.

As she pulled into a parking space in front of her gram's store, she tried not to focus on Calhoun's Feed and Seed connected here on the end of the road, allowing all the trucks to pull around to the side and back for restocking and loading. She instead looked in her rearview across the street at Ruby and Red's diner. As long as she could remember, it had been there. They were good friends with her grandmother, and Red and her granddad had been friends too. Staring in the mirror, she realized the outside had been updated with a new deep burgundy tone, similar to a mulberry, so it matched their name. That was cute, a lot better than the tan tone it had been.

She focused on her gram's store. It too had new paint, the bright tone of lemons. As if her gram had decided to show her love of the fruit. She was practically addicted to her homemade lemonade that she served to anyone who came in the store. Now the store matched her: a perky, happy lady with a spark. It was much better than it had been ten years ago, the last time she'd seen it. When she'd left, it was with the decision to never return. Oh, her grandmother had come to see her and her mom in Austin, but she had not pressed Lila to return to where her heart had been broken and her self-esteem shaken.

But here she was, only because her sweet gram needed her.

Suddenly, Lila craved a strong glass of her gram's lemonade and she let out a sigh. *She was here.* Her gaze flickered over to Calhoun's Feed and Seed. Instantly, her thoughts went to the owner's grandson Jace. Nope, not where she wanted it to go. She didn't want to think about the cowboy she had been engaged to. The man she'd trusted, until he'd had a behind-the-scenes affair…a romance with Telsie Grimes. The two of them had not gotten along because Telsie did not like that the cowboy she had a crush on was marrying Lila. It had been a shock when Telsie had told her how she and Jace had had a wonderful night. Just the thought of it now made her sick to her stomach, all these years later—and it made her really mad. Jace had declared that it wasn't true, and she had not believed him. Yes, she'd been nervous about getting married at eighteen but the details that crazy woman had told her and the fact that others had seen them together that evening, she couldn't get let go of. And then he stopped trying to get her to believe him. He'd just told her to go on with her life without him. And she'd done that.

She hadn't come back here since then. Her gram told her that he ran the ranch so his parents could enjoy traveling some and he helped his granddad out at the feed store. Not that she asked questions, but her grandmother often offered her information that she had no desire to know. She asked her gram to please leave him out of their conversation, and lately she had been doing just that. And she'd been very thankful for that. But then Gram called and needed her. She'd said she was in bad shape with her lower back hurting so that she was struggling to get up from her chair to help people when they came to the shop. Gram really needed her help. Which Lila could do, because she had an online ad designer and had the freedom move around since she could do it anywhere. She loved to travel and could do it while working. It was perfect for her to come help considering she wasn't tied down anywhere. Here she was for the first time in years, sitting here.

She looked into her rearview and saw the new dress store next to the diner that Gram had told her about. It was a soft blue, like a pale-blue sky, and it looked good. She would have to go check it out. She looked down the street, in the opposite direction from the feed store, to see whether she'd missed anymore updates and saw that most were still either old brick or faded paint; the secondhand stores still had aging paint mostly. She wondered whether they even had enough money coming in to pay for paint. She looked back at her gram's front door and sighed. It was time to get out and to quit putting off going in and worrying about what was to come. She would have to see him again considering his granddad's place was right beside her gram's, but she got out, focused on the door and nothing else, and headed toward it. This was for her sweet gram.

She had almost reached the door when she heard jingles and a loud bark and the quick clicking of dog nails, making it obvious the dog was running. She spun just as someone yelled, and then the dog was there as she faced it. It was big and jumped up on its hind legs and plastered them against her shoulders and pushed her down, he was so huge. She screamed and yelped; she was scared and turned her face away just as it licked the side of her face with its huge pink tongue. The bell on his collar jingled with each lick of his tongue—

"No," she cried, cringing just as a hand grabbed the dog's collar and pulled him off her.

"Boulder, back off. What are you doing, dog?" The man looked down at her. "I'm so sorr—"

Jace Calhoun. "Jace, what?" she gasped, stunned that he was here already. She had slobber all over her face, and the dog wiggled to get loose, lapping its tongue toward her as if it was ready to lick her other cheek. She cringed and looked back at Jace.

Jace stared at her. "Lila, I'm surprised to see you but here, let me help you up. I'm sorry about Boulder. He's a bit of a rolling stone. He doesn't normally jump up on people like that. He saw you from where we rounded the corner of the feed store and yanked so unexpectedly hard on his leash that it slid right out of my hand." He held his hand out to her.

She really didn't want to take his hand, but all she could think about was getting off the ground and getting inside the store…and washing the slobber off her face. Jace had wadded the leash up in his other hand so that the dog had to stand at his knee and couldn't get to her. She forced herself to slide her hand into Jace's and did not like the electrical voltage that shot through her from the simple touch. Their eyes locked and she wondered whether he felt it too. Instead of wondering any more, she pulled on his hand and he pulled on hers; she went to a sitting position and then to standing. Still the electrical vibration radiated through her, and she yanked her hand out of his as soon as she was on her feet.

She forced words out. "I need to wipe my face. I'm

here to see my gram. Anyway, I guess it's good to see you and your dog." Then she spun, yanked the door open, and walked inside, letting it close behind her. And she did not look back.

Her insides were shaking, and she wanted the slobber off her face. The memory of Jace's face that she'd wiped from her thoughts was now back and taking center stage. She tried to ignore him. It was time for a washing and to see her sweet grandmother.

This was not the beginning of the trip she'd envisioned…oh yes, she'd thought about seeing him again and that old memories would flow back to the front of her mind. She just hadn't expected to be plastered to the ground by his gigantic, humongous dog and get licked up one side of her face. No, this was not what she'd expected of her first moments in town. Not at all.

"Lila!"

At the shriek of her name, she looked down the center of the store to the counter and the group of chairs where friends often stopped to visit and sew or knit—

the thing her gram had enjoyed most about this store. As she'd always noted, the men gathered at Calhoun's Feed and Seed that had rougher-looking chairs sitting around a woodburning stove that in the winter months bellowed smoke from the pipe sticking out of the metal roof.

"Gram!" she squealed, unable to hold back her excitement at seeing her grandmother. Yes, there were things about this town—next door—that bothered her. But seeing her gram brought her so much joy that she rushed forward as Gram had started to push herself up out of her chair then flopped back down in it and waited for her. She reached her and bent over and hugged her tight while her grandmother squeezed her back. "It's so good to see you. How are you feeling?" She let go and bowed down beside her chair.

Gram smiled at her and cupped Lila's cheek, her soft green eyes sparkling. "Everything is better now that you're here. You know, it's just hard getting up and out of the chair. And it's hard to help customers from this chair. You came at the perfect time this morning, since Friday afternoon and Saturday are the busiest time. So you coming this morning will give you time to get ready. People love to shop on the weekend and some get a head start by getting here on Friday afternoon."

She remembered how Fridays and Saturdays were. The town might not be the greatest but people loved to leave the busy cities and come to her gram's to see what new treasures she had in. They knew that she had good taste to pick things out or refinish them in a way that would fit in their home. Many unique things were here, and even Lila was ready to explore herself, it had been so long since she'd been here. "I can't wait to see what you have. How have you been getting it done?"

"My friend who helps me on the days I go shopping for the place is still working, and I can drive and look at things and have them hauled in, so it's not too hard. But my friend Mary Lou doesn't want to work more hours, so I needed you. I wanted you to come."

She had told Lila that she really wanted to see her and even though there was a drawback next door, Lila was glad she'd come.

"Now, have a seat so we can talk."

Lila stood up and took the chair beside her gram. "Okay, go for it." She smiled.

"Your room is ready at the house. I spruced it up a little so it's more for a pretty woman than a teenager. Been needing to do that for a while."

"You didn't hurt yourself doing that, I hope."

"No. But it needed to be done, and I enjoyed it, knowing you were going to stay there again. I wanted to do it. I loved when you used to come see me. I can understand why you stopped after being hurt like that at a young adult age. Now you're here, and I'm overjoyed. And your room is fresh with things from the store that I loved and think you will too. I finally took some old toys out and I stored them upstai—well, I didn't store them upstairs. I had some help."

"I'm glad you didn't overwork. I'm here to help you, not you hurt yourself more getting ready for me. So did the doctor say anything about your hurting back? Is it your sciatica?"

"Yes, you're right. It's my sciatica and makes my back and my hips hurt. I have to do a few exercises and just be careful. Sometimes it just strikes out of nowhere and puts me down. So, just be aware of that. I'm warning you so you don't overreact if I suddenly have a problem—you know, fall down or stumble."

"Fall down!" Lila exclaimed. "You mean, you could just fall down because your back gives out?"

"Well, no, I haven't yet. I'm simply warning you in case something were to happen."

This was worse than she'd thought. Her gram falling to the floor hurt just thinking about it. The last place she wanted to see her gram was on the floor, rolling around and hurting. She was so relieved that she'd come. She clasped her gram's hand in hers. "I am here as long as you need me. I've got my online store and am blessed to be able to travel wherever I want, and this is where I want to be right now. And I can be here as long as you need me."

Gram smiled, her gentle lips curling up on the edges, and her soft green eyes twinkled. "I am so glad. It's like we are back the way we used to be."

"Not exactly, Gram. When I was younger, you were

full of all kinds of energy."

"Well, now, I do still have energy most times. This dagum back pain, or sciatica just comes and gets in my way sometimes. But don't you worry about getting bored, because I still have my regular humor coming out of these little fat lips of mine like always."

Lila laughed at the words. Her gram had always had fluffy lips, as her friends called them, and she'd gotten a lot of chuckles through the years listening to what came out of those lips. She leaned forward and gave her sweet gram a hug. This woman meant the world to her, and she was so glad she'd come. *Despite* the fellow next door.

CHAPTER TWO

Jace turned away from that door the moment Lila slammed it behind her. He couldn't believe she was finally back. Her gram had needed her. His gramps had told him that Josie Jane needed her granddaughter, and Jace knew this also because he'd gone over a few times to help her move things around or into the building when it was delivered. He would always answer to her bidding, and he would always do that as long as she needed it. But he knew that that sweet lady in there missed her granddaughter, and despite what had happened between him and Lila, he was glad she was back.

His granddaddy was standing just inside the glass door of the feed store when he pulled it opened and walked inside. From where Gramps stood, the entrance stood out with slanted windows that allowed him to stand inside while looking down the sidewalk. It had obviously given him a clear view of Jace and Lila's encounter. Jace unfastened the leash from Boulder's collar and let the large, dark silver-coated Weimaraner—or "Weim" as many who bred the large, friendly, courageous dogs called them—free. Instantly, Boulder spun toward him, making the bell on his collar ring as he looked up at Jace with his stunning blue-grey eyes. Then he cocked his head, as if trying to figure out what Jace was thinking. It was a common look, especially if there was something outside the dog wanted to chase. Now, Boulder gave a short bark, jogged back to the door, and pressed his nose to the glass, looking toward where they'd just been.

"Looks like he wants back out," Gramps said. "Something out there has his interest—how about yours?"

"I love that dog but sometimes he can get me in trouble with his spastic responses."

"You mean like jumping on your ex-fiancée and giving her a big, loving swipe of that tongue of his?"

He popped a fist to his hips and gave Gramps a firm stare. "Please don't go there. I'm might be saying please but I'm serious. Don't go there. She chose her path, accused me of stuff I can't even believe she'd believe I would do."

He walked behind the counter and could hear things being moved about on the other side of the double doors to his left. The doors led to the back side of the feed store and where his workers loaded ranchers and farmers up with whatever they needed. But right now, it was just him and his granddad. Lately, his gramps had been calling him in from the ranch more and more. He ran the ranch, which he loved doing, but growing up, he'd also loved helping Gramps run the feed store. Especially because, well, because Lila would be over there in the summertime, helping her grandma. It was always hard on him in the fall when she left their small ranch town to go back to Austin with her mom and dad and school. He'd always worked hard but looked forward to the end of a school year, when she'd return here to be with her gram. When they were old enough after high school ended, he'd asked her to marry him and they'd made big plans. But after she'd broken off the engagement because of all those ridiculous lies she'd been told, she hadn't been back.

Gramps walked to the counter and stared across it at him, a troubled expression on his face. He had told him many times to go bring that beautiful girl back. Told him to go tell her the truth and get her to believe him.

But Jace had said no. He hadn't done anything wrong. Telsie Grimes had seen him in town and said her car was broke down and would he give her a ride home. He'd told her to get one of her friends to do it but she'd begged him to do it. And like an idiot, he'd fallen for her plan. He'd carried her home and she'd tried to talk him inside for some dessert her mom had made before she'd gone to San Antonio on a shopping spree. He'd turned her down, but then she'd jumped in front of him and asked him to go out to the barn to check on a newborn calf they were having trouble with and she was worried about. That he couldn't turn down. He was good with calves and the store had a lot of medicines to help.

There had actually been a baby calf, and she'd been feeding it with a bottle. It had a cut on its leg and he'd squatted down to check on it. She'd kneeled beside him and put her hand on his knee. He'd looked at her, not having expected the touch, and then *wham!*—she leaned forward, threw her arms around his neck, and kissed him, knocking them both into the hay-strewn stall as she dug deep with her slobbery, not requested or wanted, kiss.

"What?" he'd grunted in shock as he'd pushed Telsie off him and vaulted from the hay. He'd spun and glared down at her, still shocked by what she'd done.

Her hair and eyes were big as she cocked her head to the side. "Come on, let's play. You know I like you."

He'd been furious in that moment and didn't say anything. Instead, he stomped to his truck and headed back into town. One look in the mirror, and he'd seen the fury on his face and hay in his hair. He'd been set up.

Yeah, really. She'd gone to the weekend dance the next day, the dance he'd taken Lila to, and there the conniver told her friends in front of Lila and him that he and her had a "roll in the hay at her house" and she'd loved it.

Lila had spun on him, her beautiful face screwed up in shock. "You didn't?" she'd declared.

"No, I didn't," he'd stated.

But it hadn't changed her expression as Telsie's voice could be heard behind her, singing, *"Oh yes he did."*

As if that manipulative woman was going to win him over with those kinds of lies.

The woman had lied and lied, and Lila hadn't believed his denial but instead had believed the lies. He'd stopped trying to get her back the next day, realizing that if she could believe that kind of hogwash against his truthfulness, then they had no future.

She left town, went back to Austin, and as far as he

knew, had never come back to town to see her sweet grandmother, who loved her very much. It had hurt Josie Jane, and everyone could see it, but she eventually settled with it and would travel to Austin to see her family. Still, it irritated him that Lila, the woman he'd thought he'd loved, would do that to her grandmother and also believe he'd have an affair behind her back, especially while they were committed to marriage.

So, he'd lost the woman he'd thought he'd loved, and then the woman whose lies Lila had believed started to chase him. He'd been furious and had made it clear that there had been nothing and would never be anything between them. Last he heard, Telsie had been married twice in five years and was now single again somewhere in the state.

Thinking about it now had his blood pressure rising—that Lila had believed he was like Telsie, that he was a man who thought nothing of throwing away a commitment to the woman who he'd loved and was supposed to have loved him. Nope, he wasn't. And he was going to have to get his temper back in control while she was in town.

Her gram had talked through the years, saying that Lila had a wonderful online job she loved and enabled her to travel because she could create her client's ads anywhere, anytime. He'd also caught in the tone of her voice that that place was never here with her. Then she'd looked at him one day when he was helping her move some furniture and asked him straight out whether he ever thought he might try to win her back. He'd told her in no uncertain terms that no, she had a life now and he had no desire to try to win her back after she'd believed so little in him. He hated being point-blank with her; his gramps had come into the store about that time and heard what he said. Later, in their feed store, his grandad let him have it.

Afterward, Jace had gone over and apologized to Josie Jane, and she'd hugged him.

"I so wish things had worked out, but I understand. I'm glad you're still here, at least, in my life." She'd looked up at him and her gentle green eyes had sparkled as she smiled.

He remembered that smile now and knew that he would try his hardest not to upset Josie Jane this go-round. The sweet lady did not deserve it.

He pulled his thoughts back from the past. His gramps stood across the counter, staring at him. "What? No interference, okay?"

"Jace, maybe crack that door to your heart open a little and see what happens."

"Nope, that door is slammed hard and stuck. So that's enough. Now, I've got to check somebody out," he said as the back door opened and two of the Buckley brothers walked in.

"Fine, I won't interfe—well, I'll, um, keep my mouth shut about it. Now I'll get to work." He turned, said hello to Ryder Buckley and his brother Caleb, and then he exited the double doors they'd come through.

They came to the counter. They were two of the huge family who lived on the gigantic ranch beside his small ranch. Five brothers and then two cousins lived on the ranch, too. The Buckleys loved to ranch. They did everything a ranch and farm needed. Took care of and raised cattle. Had great lakes full of fish and were always coming up with things to help the ranch be the best. He liked all of them, and they were all near the same age. Growing up, they'd all hung out together and were his friends. And they kept this feed store in business because they came here and promoted it with enthusiasm, bringing other ranchers to do business with them too. Gramps' business was booming.

And much of it was because his gramps didn't take it for granted. He got whatever they needed and kept it on hand. He worked hard to make his place reliable to any rancher who needed anything, even hard-to-get things. The business had been in their family for so long, and he knew Gramps wanted him to take over. But could he do as good a job as Gramps? He loved the ranch, too, and he had good help. Not that his ranch was anywhere near the size of the gigantic Buckley Ranch, but still, they raised great cattle. He pushed all the thoughts from his head and smiled at the brothers. He was glad to have someone break into the earlier conversation.

"Hey guys, you loaded up?"

Ryder grinned. "We're trying. We've got a trailer out there almost filled up. You've got a good group of men out there working for you."

"I agree. But you know Gramps—he likes me here at the feedstore. So, I ricochet between being a rancher and a feed store manager. And I do like the feedstore but I'm not as good at it as he is and running the ranch suits me better."

Caleb hitched a brow. "We understand. Believe us, it takes a lot of twisting and turning to keep up with our big ranching business. With you, it's a bit different because you have the smaller ranch but a feed store too. And you're good. We have no complaints."

"Thanks. I'm just like y'all—I like the ranch more."

Ryder laughed. "We understand that. And we have a whole herd of Buckleys to help control it all. We can all do our part, take breaks when we need to and know we have backups. We have choices, and so do you. You can take over and hire help to do what you do once he leaves to go do his dream of fishing night and day with Lew Potter."

"Yeah, those two fish on their day off," Caleb added. "But I think they would fish every day of their life if they had the time. The other day, we were in here and Bo was talking to Lew about going deep-sea fishing."

"In the Florida Keys, not the coast of Texas," Ryder added.

Caleb grinned. "That's a long way from here to the Keys, so they need time to drive it because you know your gramps—Bo isn't getting on a plane."

Jace chuckled. He knew about everything they were talking about. "Yep, no planes. Period."

"Well, anyway, we have to head out," Ryder said. "Send that bill to the office and West will send you the check. Thank goodness he likes the business end, because I'd hate to be stuck in there as much as he is." He grinned. "You know me—I like being on the horses and training them but will help with the cattle. But stuck behind a desk is not my calling."

"He's not lying about either of those things," Caleb said. "He'd ride a horse all day, and West…well, he wouldn't sit behind the desk all day but he does enjoy making sure we stand in the profit lane."

They all laughed because it was all true.

Jace told them goodbye then sighed. He finally had the room to himself, except for Boulder, who had actually ignored the Buckleys while he continued to stare out the window.

"Give it up, Boulder. She's not for you or for me." The dog turned his head and stared at him with his penetrating eyes. "Right, you think you know her. Well, believe me, you don't."

He'd once thought he knew her and learned the hard way he didn't. No matter what Gramps wanted or her gram…or even maybe his dog…it wasn't happening.

CHAPTER THREE

Lila had helped her gram. Well, she had made Josie Jane remain in her chair and tell her what she wanted done. She wanted prices lowered on some things, and some new things from the back needed to be moved out front and have prices put on too. She stayed busy and sweet Gram had fun telling her what to do. They laughed a lot and remembered old times. A few people had come by and she soon realized they were there to check her out because Gram had told them she was coming. Lucy Kremer and Paula May Burr were ladies she remembered for their love of hanging out and knitting with Gram. She'd smiled and hugged them and told them she was glad to see them again.

"And we're glad to see you, sweet girl," Paula May

crooned. "Your gram has missed you." She put a hand in front of her mouth so Gram couldn't see her words. "She wouldn't tell you how much," she whispered as her eyes widened for declaration.

Lucy gave her friend a "hush up" glare, then grinned at her. "We used to love you being here while we were working. You would say things that made us laugh, and you were just so sweet. It's good to have you back. Good you finally ignored what drove you away and came to visit again."

"She came to help me out," Gram broke in. "She still loves me and wanted to help."

"Yes," she managed at last. "I've been busy and the minute I heard Gram needed me, I came. And I'm sorry it took me so long." That last statement got her big smiles.

And then people from out of town started coming in to shop, and she got busy, helping them as needed. And her mind was full of regret that she'd let her foul-up in her love life keep her away from spending time with the person she loved so very much. The person who was now busy at the checkout, as more and more out-of-towners came in and began buying her products.

They were all ages—men, women, young ladies and older ladies. She loved it. Her gram had made a name for her Josie Jane's Wash and Repeat store, and she heard a lot of talk among the people as they planned to head across the road to the Mulberry Diner, owned by Ruby and Red Mulberry. Ruby was her gram's best friend and always had been. She loved being here, listening to the fun talk and helping them out. Her gram might be not getting to go pick up new things right now but there was plenty of things here to sell.

About an hour before closing, Ruby from the diner came in. "Hello there, sweet Lila. Your gram told us you were coming, and you do not know how excited we were." Ruby walked up, threw her arms wide and engulfed Lila in a tight hug. A nicely plump lady, with dark hair scattered with gray strands Ruby pulled the curly, shoulder-length curls back in a big tooth clasp that held the main part back and let small curls loose around her face. She was in her mid-sixties like her gram, and she was one strong hugger.

Lila automatically hugged her back, just as tight.

"I've missed you, Mrs. Mulberry," she said, meaning it.

"Please, I love my husband very much, but you call me Ruby. Just like you used to. Okay?"

Lila laughed and it felt so good. "Yes, Ruby. You're still as shiny as a jewel with your shining smile and fun style."

Ruby looked over Lila's shoulder and winked—at her gram, Lila assumed. Then she looked at Lila. "Yes, I have to say that most people see that in me. I kind of force them to it if not. You know if I have something funny or exciting, I like to share it. And look." She held her hand out and on it was a huge ruby ring.

"Oh goodness. That's huge! I mean beautiful," Lila blurted. The ring had to be several carats. It sparkled in the light. "Wow."

Ruby chuckled. "Red got that for me for our forty-ninth anniversary. It's a tad big." She laughed and so did Gram. "But I love it. My hubby said he tried to get one the size of his love. Isn't that sweet? And you're really enjoying it."

"Yes, I am."

Ruby wrapped an arm around her shoulder and

turned her around so they faced her gram. "So tell me, you're here and helping your gram out now. And I saw a little accident this morning from across the street at the diner's front window. I didn't come over to help because I could see right away that you were being helped by you-know-who."

Lila stalled, seeing the look on her gram's face of *what?*

And then she said it out loud. "What did you see, Ruby?"

Oh boy, here it goes.

"Well, this morning, when your sweetie arrived and got out of the car, she was coming in to see you, and she hadn't reached your door when that darling huge dog of Jace's came barreling around the corner of the feed store. And you know when Boulder likes someone he jumps up on his hind feet and props them on their shoulders—kind of an attempt at a hug. He did that to Lila and down she went with Boulder landing on top of her. That sweet dog proceeded to give her a lick on the side of the face. It was adorable. Of course, Jace came running up behind the dog, frozen at what he witnessed then quickly unfroze and pulled the dog off her. Holding Boulder back with one hand he held his free hand out to her. It was kind of romantic. How did it feel when the love of your life reached out to you today?"

Oh my goodness. Were they all going to be expecting something to happen between them? It was almost as if it had been discussed. She looked at her gram and saw the alarm on her face as she stared at her friend and gave a slight shake, as if to say hush. *Could that be true?*

Gram waved her hand. "I didn't know that happened but, really, were you hurt? That big, beautiful dog doesn't mean anything by it. But, honestly, if he likes you, he gets excited but usually Jace stops him with that leash he wears when he's out. But obviously that happened so fast this morning that he couldn't stop it. And you didn't tell me."

She rubbed her forehead, looking from Ruby to Gram. "Well…I didn't see any reason. When I came in the door, I was only thinking about you. I wasn't thinking about him or his dog…or that he'd licked my face. That's why as soon as I could, I went to the bathroom and rinsed off my face. It was to wash off all of his saliva."

Both ladies burst out laughing.

"Hey, it's not that funny. That dog slobbers a lot."

They hooted harder. Her gram slapped her leg. "Oh goodness, I truly haven't laughed this hard since you left, darlin'. I'm so glad you got greeted with love like that. If Boulder rolls you over, that's a good thing. It means he loves you."

She met her gram's eyes and suddenly wondered. "Gram, I hope you didn't invite me back here because you think something is going to happen between me and Jace."

Gram waved her hand. "No, I invited you here because I needed you. I've missed you so much, and the place hasn't been the same since you stopped coming. When my problems started up, I thought if you could come help me a little, then I could visit with you. It had absolutely nothing to do with your romance with my handsome neighbor over there and near my home too. You know, this is now, not then."

She stared at her gram and her friend, trying to

judge whether they were telling the truth. But no matter whether she had some confusion at their sweet smiles, she couldn't ignore it. Her gram really was hurt; at least, it seemed that way. She stayed in her chair all day and when she'd had to go to the restroom, Lila had walked with her. And she'd helped when she paused and seem to need steadiness. She looked between the two ladies. "I love you two. Just don't get any ideas. My past is my past, and from here on out, this is my future and has nothing to do with my past."

They both looked disappointed but nodded.

Maybe they were giving up on them finally. *Thank goodness.*

"Well, on another subject," Ruby said. "Tomorrow night is our big community dance. You'll come, right? Your gram will be ecstatic to have you with her. Everyone who hasn't seen you in all these years will be excited to see you too."

"I was going to invite you, but Ruby beat me. We are going, right?"

Lila stared from one to the other. She could turn this down, considering she'd just gotten here, but her gram looked absolutely happy at the thought. "Sure, I'll go. I want to see everyone also. Will there be a lot of people there?"

Ruby grinned. "Oh yes. And I know you probably remember all the Buckley brothers and their two cousins who live on the huge ranch right outside of town. They'll be there. Several of them were in the diner for breakfast this morning, and I asked them. They smiled those amazing smiles they have and assured me they wouldn't miss it. Do you remember them? I mean, you were always infatuated with…well, the one we aren't going to mention anymore. But all those Buckleys have grown up and are amazingly handsome and *single*. I know, I know—you probably aren't interested in anything like that while you're here for your gram. But this town has a lot to offer when it comes to single cowboys. We're a small town and there are not that many girls your age. But we have a new ladies store beside the diner, and the owner's single and really nice. You'll have to go over and meet Genna Barry. She's about your age. And you'll love her clothes. It is so wonderful. At first, it was a little bit too young for me but she ordered this especially with me in mind and has been getting things in for me ever since. My Red loves me in more bright colors instead of my jeans and simple T-shirts that I used to wear."

Lila remembered her black and tan outfits, and she had to agree Ruby now looked like bright sunshine, which matched her personality. "You look wonderful. I was just thinking how that frothy-looking yellow blouse matches your happy and uplifting personality."

"Aw, that is so sweet. I like this new look myself. And not that you need a new look—you always look great, with your cute and pretty clothes—but go over and meet Genna. I have a feeling you'll like each other."

Gram nodded from her chair. "I do too. But she might beat you and come over here. I've told her about you, and she wants to meet you."

"With these raves about her, I'll go meet her tomorrow, if there is time between the influx of customers you have on Saturdays. I bet she's busy too."

"She will be," Gram said. "But she'd like to meet you, and I can give you a few minutes off tomorrow." Gram laughed at her words, and Lila and Ruby did too.

"I love this." She looked from one to the other. "I've missed this."

And she had.

* * *

At six o'clock, Jace had locked up the store. His granddad had left early to go fishing at one of the many ponds he went to with his buddy Lew. So Jace locked the front door, then exited through the side area, making sure the leash was connected to Boulder's collar before heading outside. And he did not let go. And thank goodness, because the animal walked out the door and then jumped into what would have been a full run toward the front of the store. But Jace instantly held tight and drew him back.

He'd stood at the window all day, not at attention but he'd sunk down on his rear and kept his eyes down the sidewalk to the store next door. And about closing time for Josie Jane's store, Boulder barked and stood, his nose to the glass.

He suspected the dog saw Lila, by his reaction. He

kept glaring over at the checkout desk where Jace was working, as if telling him to get over there and let him outside. His dog obviously liked Lila.

Well, there had been a time when he'd been just like his dog, full of excitement at the prospect of seeing her. He hadn't wiggled like Boulder but his heart did pound and his adrenaline rushed the moment he saw her and took her into his waiting arms. But she'd killed that. And it had been tough to get used to the idea that she wasn't the right woman for him, but a woman who wouldn't believe him when he'd not done anything wrong. He'd managed to let her go because her attitude had hit deep and angered him so. But still, he hadn't found anyone so far he would consider marrying. He wasn't sure whether it was because she'd really messed with his head and heart and he never wanted to go through that again, or—and he didn't want to even think it—it could be that he never truly got over her.

It was irritating. He wanted to settle down. He had a nice sized ranch, not anywhere near the monster-sized ranch of the Buckley Ranch. But it was a great size; did just enough cattle to keep him busy and make a profit.

And the times when he didn't make a profit, they had the feed store. That place did a huge business. It might not look like some of the fancy new places in the bigger surrounding areas, but it had a homey feeling that all his customers seemed to enjoy, and continually came back again and again. And that was why he worried that if he took over, they could lose some of the atmosphere that his granddaddy's presence put in that place. Just the way he handled people was magic, and people loved him. He wasn't sure he had the gift of drawing people to the feed store. Would they keep coming if his granddad wasn't there? Or if he did take over and got someone to kind of take over the store so he could spend more time at the ranch that he loved, what would that do? Would the store still keep its high-level reputation? His gramps had told him over and over that they provided a great service, kept everything their customers needed or would need in stock, and if they didn't have it, they got it in as soon as possible.

He had to keep telling himself that his gramps believed in him. He glanced over at the white older house as he and Boulder passed by. It sat on a small ten-acre stretch of land that edged his larger property and that was where Lila's gram had lived all of her married life with her husband. And now, as he glanced at it, he saw Lila's red Jeep sitting in the circle drive in front of the white house. He yanked his head forward and stared straight ahead.

Two miles down the road, he turned onto his family's long drive and drove up the white rock to the main house. The house he had taken over when his mom and dad had moved into the smaller home on down the road that they used as their station in-between their traveling. And his gramps had never lived in that house that Jace's mom and dad built when they married. He lived farther back, between two ponds on the ranch, in a pretty big cabin that he loved. The ranch wasn't gigantic but it had everything they all needed.

He drove behind the main house and parked inside the garage. The barns and stables were across the large gravel area at least half the distance of a football field. He cut the truck off, stepped out of the truck, and then unhooked the dog's leash so he had freedom.

Instantly, Boulder dove from the truck and raced

toward the stables. Halfway there, he spun around and looked at Jace.

"I'm coming. Believe me, I need a ride just like you need a run of freedom, hunting for mole holes and digging for the irritating little creatures. Burn some of your energy off before we go inside." He walked into the stable where he kept his main horse. It had an entrance to the small connecting pasture that enabled him to enjoy the outside when he wanted to.

Hearing him coming, Cinder waited at the stall gate, his head sticking out over the gate. He whinnied the moment he saw Jace.

"Yep, I'm glad to see you, too, big fella. Ready for some exercise?"

In answer Cinder threw his head upward and gave a loud whinny and started to paw the dirt he stood on.

"Okay, hang on, buddy. I'm ready for a ride too. Need to get my brain on something other than what it's been stuck on all day." It was true; she had kept breaking into his thoughts all day long. Really irritating, but she was there. He ignored the stirring in the pit of his stomach and pushed it away. He would not go there. He would not.

He grabbed his saddle blanket and his harness, then entered the stall. Within moments, he had the horse ready for a ride. He led it out the back of the stall and for the fence. He opened the gate and then climbed into the saddle. Boulder was romping around beside them his excitement showing because he knew they were fixing to roam. The moment Jace gave the horse permission to go, the dog let out an excited bark and took off at lightning speed ahead of them.

Cows in the pasture barely raised their heads at the dog, used to the excited exercise the dog had to have every day. He remembered when he fell in love with the little dog and looked it up on the internet; it had clearly pointed out that the Weimaraner needed an owner who liked exercise because this dog breed were friendly, family-type dogs but needed activity and lots of it. Jace hadn't hesitated and had bought the pup because he'd already been won over by the way it cocked his head to the side and those light-blue eyes that changed to gray-blue as he aged. He brought Boulder home, having named him right after buying him because the puppy was so excited, it had tumbled over and rolled across the floor like a small boulder. The name had been perfect. He'd taken Boulder through a great training program to help them learn each other and help him know what exactly the pup needed to grow healthy and happy. It turned out they had similar personalities, both needing time outside to release stress and to get an abundance of exercise.

Now, he directed Cinder to the right, knowing the lake they were headed toward was close to Lila's grandmother's home. They wouldn't be seen from their house because the hill around the small lake hid him, even on a horse. He just had to get over the ridge quickly, and all would be good. He could have gone to the right, through several fences to other small lakes, and he'd be near the Buckleys' ranch, but this was easier—less fences to open and the gentle peace that came from riding the horse slowly around the lake as Boulder had a romping great time. Instantly, thoughts of him and Lila having good times there at the lake reared up in his head.

Yep. She'd climb the fence and jog over there from

her gram's, and meet him over the hill beside the glistening water. He really didn't want his mind going to those meetings but it was too late. When they were young, they'd fish and have a good time. She loved to fish and he did too. And then when they were between their eighth grade and ninth grade was when he gave in to what he'd been dreaming of for a long time. He leaned in while she was laughing because she'd caught a bigger fish than him, and he'd kissed her. She'd stopped laughing, stood still, their gazes locked, and then she'd smiled broadly, leaned forward and kissed him back.

They'd been a couple from that day forward. He'd loved her from early on…boy, how he had misunderstood things. He'd thought she'd loved him but at the first stinking lie that came along between them, she'd believed it. And he hadn't been able to let it go.

He topped the hill and looked across the distance at the house on the other side of the fence. He paused, staring for just a second before urging the horse to a quicker pace down the hill where no one from the house could see him. Boulder was already tramping through the shallow water, making splashes that made the dog grin and snap at the water splashing around him. He barked, not that he barked a lot but just when he liked something or someone or loved something, and Boulder loved this spot.

Just like Jace always had. *And Lila.*

Why was he thinking these thoughts? Why was he letting himself go there?

He hadn't allowed himself to think about Lila in a very long time. Yes, when it had all first happened, he had let her go and reprimanded himself about it for a long time. Many people questioned him, including his granddad. His parents had questioned him too, but Gramps had been the main one. Telling him that sometimes important things needed to be fought for and asking him whether he was sure he was right. He'd been mad at Gramps for a while but gotten over it. Gramps had stopped asking him about it all and never mentioned it in the last few years, and things had pretty much gone back to normal. Except that Lila had stopped coming to town.

He paused the horse beside the water and lay the

reins down, yanked his Stetson from his head, and stared out across the tranquil water. The calmness did nothing to still the reeling waves of misery that he'd once felt and raced forward for the first time in a very long time. He glared at the sun setting on the horizon, feeling in the moment the same heat that radiated from the sun. He shifted his gaze to the lake where Boulder raced through the water, knee-deep with a huge grin on his face as his short tail wagged like a drummer banging out a fast tempo. His large ears flopped to the tempo and he let out a bark. The dog loved running and water; this was his perfect place.

Just like it had once been Jace's favorite place, with only great memories and future hopes. His and Lila's.

"Why in the heck did you come out here today?" he muttered out loud, jerking Boulder's attention to him.

The dog eyed him and then let out a loud bark, as if to say, "You did it for me."

And he had. Boulder had no idea that he used to come out here with someone else.

CHAPTER FOUR

There was a loud sound in the distance as she walked out onto Gram's back porch. Gram sat in the den, resting, as Lila prepared them a small pot of coffee. Only one cup each because neither of them wanted anything to keep them awake. So while she waited for it to brew, she'd walked outside and heard the sound. She heard it again; this time, it was clearly a bark. Her gaze was instantly riveted to the ridgeline of a small hill on the other side of the fence. The fence that boarded her gram's property and Jace's property.

There was a beautiful though small lake on the other side of the ridge. Many would call it a large pond, but it was bigger than a pond and she always called it a lake. And so had Jace. They had both loved that lake and met there often.

Was Jace with his dog at the lake? She'd thought about sneaking over there while she was here to see it. It was beautiful and, well, she had memories there that she didn't want to think about, but she'd loved that lake. So, on a day when she thought he wasn't home, she would cross over for a moment. There was a spot that, if she walked down the fence of her gram's property where the ridge almost disappeared, she'd see a large portion of the lake. She could go in that way and could make sure no one was there. *Great.* That plan in place, she went back into the house and poured two coffees. Later they'd have dinner, and she and Gram would talk a little more and then bedtime. She would be ready because she had to prepare for a day of work at the store and then the party. The party that meant if she hadn't seen him at work again—and she hoped that was the case—then she would see him at the dance, because there was no getting out of her being there.

Who would he be with?

The thought sprang to her mind, and she almost gasped as she picked up the coffee cups. *She didn't care who he would be with at the party. She didn't care at all.*

* * *

Jace pulled into town the next morning, just before six a.m. when the diner officially opened. Boulder had turned instantly and smashed his nose to the rear window looking across the street—not at the feed store but at Josie Jane's Wash and Repeat and that was where Jace left him as he got out and entered Mulberry Diner.

"Good morning." Red Mulberry beamed from behind the counter. "I was expecting you. Your regular? Coffee and an egg muffin to go?"

He walked up to the counter of the empty diner that would soon be filled with its regulars and weekend customers. "That would be great. I've got a ton of work to get done, and Gramps is fishing today so he won't be in to hassle you." He slid onto one of the barstools and gave chuckle as Red laughed.

"He doesn't hassle me, at least not like he hassles you. Lew go with him?"

"That's true. And yep, Lew is with him. They headed out to the back side of the ranch yesterday to evening fish, camp out, and start fishing early this morning."

"So you're opening today. Going to the dance tonight, right?" Ruby beamed brightly as she walked from the kitchen, carrying a large plate of what looked like blueberry muffins. She slid open the back of a glass display and placed the dish of muffins on the second row among several other plates of muffins.

"Yes, ma'am. I'll be there."

Instantly, Red and Ruby smiled at the same time, their gazes meeting.

Jace inhaled slowly, his fear coming to light. His Gramps wasn't the only one thinking there was still hope between him and Lila.

"It'll be a good dance," Red said. "I'll get your egg muffin ready."

"I'll get your coffee." Ruby turned and reached for a large paper cup. "Josie Jane is thrilled to have Lila back in town after all this time. I saw you and that sweet dog of yours out front yesterday." She turned toward him, grinning hugely as she carried the filled cup to the counter and set it in front of him. "I loved it. It was a memorable first meeting you two had after such a long time. I think, by the way Boulder was acting, that he instantly liked her a lot."

Everyone knew that Boulder jumping meant he liked you. And with the power of that jump, he figured Ruby was taking that for downright love at first sight for his dog. The fact that Boulder jumped to his feet and focused on where he'd tackled Lila the day before had Jace's head thumping now. "He just got carried away and took me off guard. I lost his leash and couldn't catch him before he rounded the corner and headed straight for her."

"I saw that. And it was nice of you to help her up. Were you shocked to see her after all these years?"

He rubbed his chin, an itch of discomfort seeping in. He glanced toward the kitchen. "Sure. It has been a while, but she seems fine." She had not liked seeing him that was for certain.

"And still as pretty as always."

Thank goodness Red came out of the kitchen, carrying his bag, and passed it to him. "Thanks, you two." He stood and handed over the money. "Keep the change. I need to go get busy. Y'all have a great day."

And then he headed to the door and made it to his truck right before the early morning rush hit. They started arriving as he drove across the street and turned down the side road beside his feed store. He'd gotten out just in time. He hadn't even thought about the talk that Lila returning would stir up.

He parked and quickly snapped the leash on Boulder because he was at alert and ready to spring from the truck. Securing the dog leash in his hand, he opened the door and instantly Boulder dove across him, missing him and the steering wheel, and landed on the ground— and would have gone farther had he not had on the leash. Smart dog knew this but still wanted on the ground, waiting for him to get out and obviously follow him down the street, where he was pointing with his nose and body.

"Nope, not going today." *This was ridiculous.* Jace grabbed his bag and cup of coffee and followed the dog out, shutting the door with his hip before heading to the side entrance as his dog strained to head toward the front sidewalk and—he was certain—straight to the doorway where he'd knocked her down and gave her a lick of love.

She had drawn his dog's attention and, as much as he wanted to deny it, she had drawn his once more. He admitted that he'd hardly slept last night because of the beautiful woman. He hadn't meant to think *beautiful woman*, but that's what came up automatically when thoughts of her entered his brain. As maddening as it was, that was how it was. She'd kept his mind occupied last night. When he went to sleep, his thoughts instantly journeyed back to years ago, when she'd consumed his life and filled him with joy. He'd fought his way awake several times last night, though one time he was shaking so hard, he'd sat up in bed sucking in deep breaths. Thinking about her had him reliving a hopeful time filled with love. A time he'd forced himself to let go of though it had been a fight to push the dreams of a life with her away; obviously, the inside fight was trying to reappear now that she was back in town.

He pushed away the thoughts, opened the door, and tugged Boulder inside, feeling as if he were fighting an actual huge boulder rolling the other way as the dog tugged to go down the street. He managed to get the animal inside and closed the door, then headed to the door leading into the front store. Once he released the leash, Boulder raced to the front window and took up his watch for Lila to arrive.

Taking his concentration off the dog, Jace went to work, preparing to open the store. After he had the register ready, he glanced toward the front window where Boulder had his front paws on the low windowsill, his tongue hanging out to the left, and his eyes drilled to the area down the sidewalk from where he stood. There was no doubt who the dog was waiting for.

Jace headed out the back door, leaving the dog inside. His workers would be here any moment and also ranchers and farmers needing feed and seed and who knew what else. His gramps made sure they had it all. He opened the large gate and slid it open as trucks began to turn onto the side lane and parking. His helpers were getting out of their vehicles and told him good morning as they entered the yard and headed toward the platform, ready to carry out whatever the customers needed. Saturdays were usually busy and by the looks of the trucks, it would be today too. He headed back into the front of the store to be prepared to check everyone out when they were finished getting supplies.

And there was Boulder, still sitting at the window. *The dog had it bad.*

* * *

Saturday, Lila rode into town with Gram in her granddad's old truck that he'd redone years ago. Gram loved the truck—always drove it to town and parked it in front of the store because she loved that it had belonged to the man she'd loved for so many years and because it represented the same thing her store did—that old things weren't trash but treasures.

Gram pulled into the front parking space and as she shut the engine off, Lila caught movement to her right and looked over at the feed store's angled windows and front door. There was the large dog. His feet were on the bottom of the window frame and as she opened the door of the truck, the large, thin-legged but muscled dog sprang suddenly to his hind legs, placing his front feet on the midsection of the window, and barked.

She looked over the hood of the truck at Gram, who looked a bit shocked as she, too, stared at the dog. "I think he must like your truck."

"That is the first time I've ever seen Boulder standing at the window like that. Honestly, that dog has seen me drive up here many times and just stands there and watches me. But that? Goodness, he's got his front paws on the top half of the window and he's wiggling like he's wagging that short tail of his at a hundred miles an hour. I think if he could, he'd bust that door open and come racing out here and jump on you again."

Lila stared at the dog. "You really think he's doing that because of me?"

"Look at that big grin on his face and the way he keeps flopping that long tongue that's hanging out of his mouth from one side to the other. I don't think he likes you—I think he likes you a *lot*."

Lila chuckled, watching him. That big dog had taken her down yesterday, then tried to lick her down, and then kept trying to come back to get at her again. "I wonder what makes him like me like that?"

"Maybe he just knows a great young woman when he sees her." Gram hitched a brow at her then walked to the front door of the shop. She shot a grin over her shoulder as she inserted the key. "He might be trying to tell his owner something."

She stared at her gram and got a grin from her before she entered the building and left Lila standing there. She wanted to tell her grandmother there was nothing to tell, but she was already gone. The dog barked again, plopped down onto his front feet, and rocked his head from one side to the other, as if beckoning her over. Unable to stop herself, she stepped up onto the sidewalk and walked over to the window, touching her fingers to the window. The dog instantly planted his nose to the glass.

"Well, you cutie, I guess you do like me, huh?" She chuckled and for a moment even thought about going into the building and petting him. But that wasn't happening. And then she looked up from the dog, and there stood Jace. He looked startled to see her and probably was, having most likely come to see what was causing all the ruckus from the excited dog. And he was probably disappointed to find it was her again. She thought about turning away but instead she walked to the front door as he did too. He reached for the dog's collar to hold it back as he opened the door for her, and she walked inside. They were going to be around each other while she was here, so they might as well get on speaking terms, overlook what happened between them and move forward.

"I have to say, your dog surprises me but he is also very friendly, and I thought I'd come and pet him. Gram says his name is Boulder." She looked at the wiggling dog. It was big but not gigantic. His shoulders were almost to Jace's thighs, and Jace was tall—about six foot two, if she remembered right. The dog was slim but had a wide chest and was pure muscle with lean legs that enabled him to spring instantly to his back legs and slap his front paws to Jace's shoulders. But to her five-foot, eight-inch shoulders, his paws had hung over her shoulders and the weight and momentum had tilted her off-balance and then to the ground.

Not today though, as Jace held him back.

"Yes, his name is Boulder, as you've seen why," he chuckled. "Sorry about that. And yes, you can pet him. I've got him. He knows commands but at the moment he's not listening to them. He has a highly enthusiastic temperament when you are around. Pet him and see if he calms down."

She reached out both hands, placed one hand on the side of his neck and the other she placed on his forehead between his big ears, and rubbed gently. The dog's tongue instantly sagged out of its mouth to the right as it leaned into the pressure to get as much contact from her hand as it could get. His beautiful eyes closed, and she grinned widely, unable to not smile. This dog was amazing. "I've never been overwhelmed by a dog before but he's wonderful. I mean, what kind is he?"

"Boulder is a Weimaraner. The short name for that is a 'Weims.' They are large, highly and I mean *highly* energetic. The warning on the dog charts are basically if you don't want or like exercise, don't get this dog. They're happy, athletic, love to snuggle and connect with their owner and family, but above all, they love exercise and need it. If they don't get it, they will likely entertain themselves in other ways as in tearing things up about the house to use up their energy. So it's a warning that is indeed true—if you aren't going to get them out and about, this is not the dog someone wants. You know how I am—the moment I saw him as a puppy and heard the details, I knew he was perfect for me. I like to be outdoors and if I'm not here helping out Gramps, then I'm out herding cattle, roaming the land, checking fences or down by a lake."

She smiled because what he said was what she already knew about him, and the dog fit him perfectly. "You sound like a good match."

"Yep. He's not a cow dog but he can run them. He loves hunting and he's particularly drawn to anything that digs holes in pastures, especially moles whose holes and tunnels can cause problems for cattle, horses, and people. But mostly he likes to swim in the ponds and lakes, race along the shoreline—or anywhere, actually. And chasing things like raccoons, possums, and more give him the time of his life, running and zigzagging across the land." He smiled at her. "Until yesterday, I didn't know he also likes to chase women. Still sorry about that."

His lips tilted up in a sparkling smile as she looked up at him. Her heart jerked but despite that she couldn't help grinning too as she rubbed Boulder's large ears. Ears that were actually bigger than her hands. She focused on the dog as he cocked his head from one side to the other while she rubbed his short, silver-gray hair. His sparkling blue-grey eyes locked onto hers as he moved his head, trying to get her to rub harder. His tongue again hung out, and he tried then to lick her wrist.

She laughed and managed to shift her wrist to miss the lick. "I can see how the two of you fit in well with each other."

It was true. Jace was over-energetic, always out in

the pastures, working hard at building fence or working cattle; he explored on horseback, or he was fishing. Then there were times she remembered well when he was running across the pasture on his own feet, chasing her as she laughed and pushed herself to run and beat him to a targeted tree. She hadn't minded one bit when he would catch her and they'd tumble to the ground, laughing. She tried not to let those thoughts continue but they were there. She took a deep breath of air, kept the special dog's head between her hands, and did not look up at Jace. No way could she let him see what she felt her eyes could be saying if they locked with his deep brown penetrating eyes.

"You're a good dog, Boulder, and obviously good at keeping your guardian here busy. Now, I need to go work. Keep your buddy busy and out of trouble." The last words came out before she realized it, and her gaze shot to Jace. She took a step back to the door. "Anyway, just thought it would be good to come over and get to know Boulder. In all honesty, Jace, I was pretty rude yesterday. But it was mostly from being startled by Boulder and then you. I know we have a past, but I moved away from it a long time ago. So maybe we just start from scratch, be friends while I'm here taking care of Gram and just pretend all that other stuff never happened. It obviously wasn't meant to be."

He didn't move; he'd been lightly smiling and now his dark gaze shifted, as if digging into her thoughts. Thoughts she did not want him digging into at this moment.

"You don't have to answer that," she blurted. "I'll go back to the store—"

"No, wait. I just wasn't expecting you to say that. But you're right. Your gram needs you and has missed you a lot. And…so, yeah, we can be friends. And forget about the past. But I have a feeling that there are a lot of people who haven't forgotten about it. Anyway, just a warning."

"You mean like my gram and Ruby?"

"Exactly. I just have a feeling that they don't want us to not go back in time."

She reached out and rubbed Boulder's forehead because the dog was straining against the hand holding it back by its collar. "Well, I'm actually glad to be here.

I've missed the town and the people. But they don't have any ideas, do they?"

"You mean about us?"

She saw the way his eyes flickered at that word. "Yes," she said. "Because there is no *us*. Hasn't been for all these years, and won't be ever again." She had to say that because of the momentary look she'd seen in his penetrating brown eyes. She needed him to know she had not come back to try to start something up between them. Even though she'd suddenly gotten that vibe yesterday; now, after he wondered about it, she needed to make it plain and clear. But she had a sneaking suspicion that Gram and Ruby might have other ideas.

"You're fine. I'm not going to bother you. I'll try my best to keep my dog away from you. If somehow, he gets loose and comes running at you and you see him plowing toward you, sternly say 'Down.' Okay?"

She nodded. "I will. Okay, time to work. Gram says Saturdays are still as busy as they used to be, so since she's sitting in a chair, I need to go make sure everything is ready. And like I had to yesterday, I need to make sure she's staying in her seat."

She opened the door and walked out.

"If you need anything, I'm right here," he called. "I know Gram has a strong mind and might do what she wants, so let me know."

She looked back at him. "Thanks, I will. Yes, Gram has always done what she wants and if she sees something on a shelf that a customer wants and I'm busy with something else, she might try. So, I'll be on alert and may have to call you. Thanks, that would be like the old days, wouldn't it?"

He chuckled and the sound rang through her, just like it used to. "Yeah, brings back a lot of memories."

She tugged the door closed and without looking back, she headed away. Behind her, she heard the dog bark as memories she wasn't wanting to think about raged into the forefront of her thoughts.

CHAPTER FIVE

Jace lowered the tailgate of his truck, exposing the rectangle-shaped galvanized watering tank sitting in the bed. His friend Zack Buckley reached for one hand grip on his end and Jace grabbed the one on his end, and they pulled it to the tailgate. They had brought it from the feed store to be used for the night at the community center Spring Fling. It was to be used as an ice tank for cold drinks tonight and then back to the store to be sold as a watering trough or whatever someone wanted to use it for.

Instead of lifting the tank from the tailgate, Jace looked at his friend. "You're not dating anyone, are you?" Zack didn't date often and Jace had heard a rumor that he might be dating someone.

"No. I don't know who started that rumor but it's not true. I don't have time to be dating right now and like you, I'm not interested. Once you get burned to the core, it's hard to get back to it. You know it as well as I do that sometimes getting back to dating is just not in the cards."

Boy, did he know. And that was why he'd been curious about the rumor he'd heard today at the feed store about his good friend. After what had happened to him the day before he was supposed to marry Lila, Jace hadn't dated much. He and Zack had different situations but the same outcome of being alone. Zack had walked in and found his fiancée with another cowboy and had completely shoved ever trying it again to the curb.

Jace sighed. "I know what you mean. I tried dating some, but gave up fast, not trusting that if I put my heart back out there, it wouldn't get trampled again." Zack was the only person who he'd tell that much truth to about how he'd felt about Lila believing the worst about him.

Zack shifted the weight of the tank. "Me either. I figure if I ever do fall in love again, it will be with someone who just walks in the door and sweeps me off my feet or knocks me to the ground—it would have to be something earth-shaking because I just don't feel interested in putting myself out there anymore. So, I heard Lila was back in town. Are you okay?"

He hitched a shoulder. "She's back helping out her gram, but that doesn't mean anything to me."

"Hey, you know I was around when all that went on, and I was your best man. I saw how it affected you, and I've watched you over the years, pulling back from connecting with anyone. And like I said, I understand. But I can't help but wonder after all this time how you're feeling."

Pressure that had been building in him all day since seeing Lila this morning in his store now pounded up and he slapped a hand to his thigh. "You know, it was tough having her believe such crazy things about me back then, when I thought she knew me. You know, I talked to you about it. I thought she loved me. I thought she knew me and then at the first hint that I was having an affair with—well, Lila packed up and headed out and never returned. Yeah, you could say I'm a little unforgiving at this point. But she came in this morning to talk to me." He did not miss the look of happiness on his friend's face. "Hey, don't be looking like that."

"Sorry. I know I said I'm like you. But I really thought you two were perfect together. Like everyone else, I thought it was sad when y'all split like that. But I understand what you're saying. She loved you and then to just not believe you—yeah, I'm with you. I'd probably have had a hard time forgiving her, too, for believing the lies about you." He paused then leaned his head to the side and his gaze dug deep. "So, she really came into the feed store today?"

"She came inside to pet Boulder. The day before, he yanked away from me getting out of the truck then raced around the building. I tried to hang on to him but he was gone in a flash around the building, and as I made it around the building behind him he'd pounced on a woman, it was Lila. It was as if he sensed something he liked and he went and found her. He'd thrown his arms to her shoulders like he likes to do and had her on the ground. He was licking her on the side of her face when I got to them. I got him off her. You should have seen the look on her face when she saw who had pulled him off her. And no telling what I looked like, seeing her for the first time in all these years. Completely not who I was expecting when I pulled him off."

Zack had started laughing. "Wow. I can only imagine."

"Yeah, it wasn't pretty—well, you know, she was not happy in the first place and then she saw me, and it just got worse. We said a few words, I don't even remember what; then frowning she went inside. Which was fine with me, I wasn't wanting to stand out there and talk either. It was kind of hard. Then, this morning, the dog was standing at the front window, watching for her. I could tell the moment she drove up. That dog went crazy. She walked over to the window to look at him, probably out of curiosity, and it was about the time I went to see if in fact Boulder was looking at who I thought and there we were staring at each other." He shook his head and paused remembering that moment.

He met Zack's penetrating stare again. "When she saw me, instead of turning away she startled me by coming to the door and entering the store."

"Interesting," Zack cooed.

"Hey, hypothetically it was to pet the dog…*then* to tell me that we needed to forget what happened and basically be friends while she's here in town. Pointing out that our grandparents need us and don't need our history putting any pressure between them."

"Wow. And you said?"

Jace's brows slammed together. "I agreed with her. What else was I supposed to do?"

"Don't go getting mad. So, y'all have agreed to not hold your past against each other?" Zack rested his elbow on the edge of the tank and leaned his cowboy-hatted head to the side, drilling him with his eyes.

"Yeah, that's what we agreed to…I mean…I can't not do that because she did need to come here and see her gram and she needs to make it a habit. Her gram misses her. Having something between us that she obviously didn't care about getting to the bottom of then or now—well, it just needs to be swept under the log pile and us move on."

"You didn't say something in all those words you

just said to me that is very important."

Jace gave his friend a glower. "And what are you saying?"

"I'm saying you didn't say you *wanted* to do that. You said y'all *needed* to do that. You're my friend, my buddy, and I think you still care for her. And she's in town, so why not take advantage of that and see if things have changed?"

His heart pounding Jace looked toward the pasture that connected to the area here at the back of the community building. His mind swirled and he tried to get rid of the ideas that Zack's words brought to the surface. He didn't want to go there. Couldn't go there.

"Come on, man. *Talk to me*," Zack encouraged him.

He stared at his friend then spoke the words out loud as much for himself as for Zack, "I *can't* go there. She thought something terrible of me. She broke up what was supposed to be the happiest time in our life because she thought the worst of me. How am I supposed to even test the waters of that ever again?"

Zack broke into a smile instantly. "Because you're Jace Calhoun, that's why. Look, what I said a few minutes ago about you and me being similar…well, there is a difference. I know what *you-know-who* did to me. There was no guessing; it was right there in front of me when I opened that door and found her with him. No way could she deny what was going on and she didn't— no, she laughed about it. Emotionally, at that time, I think you felt what I felt, but the proof isn't there for Lila like it was for me. She has no proof that you did what my ex did. And you don't even know…maybe she's questioning that finally. If she's not questioning it, maybe you need to talk to her and make her understand that what she thought happened didn't. And never could have because you only wanted her in your life, as your wife and love. And I think maybe you still want her, love her. Okay, so I just needed to put that in your head since I had put other stuff in there too. Come on, let's get this tub in there. I'm with you one way or the other— just wanted to run that by you."

Jace lifted his end of the tub up. "Yeah, let's do this. And thanks. I know you didn't say it to bother me. We'll see. Maybe I do need to think about it. I did agree to get along. So, anyway, let's get this inside. And then maybe you and me both need to commit to dancing a little bit tonight—at least to one dance with someone new, instead of us standing around on the sidelines like we always do, watching everyone else dancing. We used to be out there with them. So what do you think—at least one dance with someone?"

Zack started to carry his end toward the entrance. "I don't know, I might... Tell you what...if I dance a dance with someone and you do the same, we can at least say we gave it a try."

Jace grinned. "Deal. I'll do it and you'll do it. We're grown up and we can live through a dance."

He'd lived through enough, but could he really test the waters and see whether Lila might believe him after all these years?

* * *

The band was practicing as Lila looked at her watch. She'd just set a case of sodas on the table that would be beside the metal trough they would use to ice down all the can drinks. She had been helping get the drinks ready as she waited for the container to be delivered that would hold the good assortment of non-alcoholic drinks for everyone. She loved that it was that way, because it was a gathering for all ages. If anyone wanted alcohol, they had to bring it, and it wasn't allowed inside. It was fine with her; she didn't drink much, maybe a glass of champagne on special occasions but normally she was a water with lemon drinker or a morning coffee drinker. She didn't look down on those who liked a drink but this dance wasn't just for grownups; they had kids young and old—toddlers to teenagers. It was a fun event. She remembered it when she was younger, automatically looking across the table toward the dance floor. She saw the lights were still similar, hanging down so they would sparkle when the music played. Instantly, the memory of the first time she'd danced with Jace here on that dance floor flooded her mind.

She spun away from the dance floor and found herself seeing the rear door and none other than Jace entering the building. He was helping carry in the container she was waiting on. Their gazes met and a sudden jolt of electricity shot through her as if she'd been struck by lightning. She lost her breath, it was so powerful. She tried to yank her eyes from his but they were stuck, as if the electric jolt had melted their eyes together. Her skin tingled and her stomach wavered. *This was not good. Oh, so not good.*

"Hey there, Lila. I heard you were in town." His buddy helping him carry the trough grinned at her and because they were approaching her with the trough between them, they both had a view of her.

Thank goodness her gaze let go of Jace and went to his helper. "Zack Buckley, how are you?" she asked with a laugh, as much from relief as from seeing him. Hoping he or Jace hadn't noticed her frozen gaze that had been stuck on Jace.

Zack grinned, obviously having noticed. "I'm doing good. And you're looking good. Now, just tell us where you want this."

"End of the table. And then I'll bring the ice in—"

"No, no," Zack said. "We'll get the ice and bring it in while you get the sodas all freed up and ready for a cold dip. In thirty minutes, when everyone gets here, they'll be nice and chilled." He set his end of the tub on the ground, and then while Jace got his on the ground, Zack reached out and pulled her into a hug. "It's good to see you. It's been too, too long. Hope you have a good evening, it's gonna be a fun night." He let her go, grinned at her, and then headed toward the kitchen.

Jace remained at the end of the tub looking uneasy, just like she felt.

She raked a hand through her hair. "Thank you, Jace. Y'all really don't have to carry the ice in."

He leaned his head toward the kitchen. "He was right. You don't have to carry all that ice in here. We volunteered to help, so we'll do it. And I'm sure your grandmother is happy you're helping. Is she sitting down somewhere?"

She nodded toward the kitchen, her lips curving up. "She's sitting at the table in there, making some kind of appetizer with cheese and tortillas…I think, anyway…things like that…and her and Ruby are just talking up a storm. I don't know if those two ever stop talking when they are together."

He chuckled. "I know what you mean. That's some kind of strong friendship those two have. This whole town is built up through their friendship. I mean, I have tons of memories involving those two. Having fun like this with them, making sure everyone is fed well and having a good time, like this dance. And if you're sick, they'll make sure you get fed. Gramps says they have always done things to help everyone, even behind the scenes. They're good, and I'm glad to help them get this party going, even if it's just bringing a bucket and some ice." He grinned and her pulse scrambled again.

"Two of a kind," she managed and focused on Gram and Ruby, not the way her pulse was racing. "A wonderful kind and encouraging ladies. I really missed them. And it's going to be a good evening just watching them sit in chairs beside these refreshment stands and talk to anyone and everyone who wants to stop and say hello."

"You're right. And Gramps will be here soon, and he fits right in there with them. Him and some of his buddies. Those two stand out. Anyway, glad we got to talk just a minute. I hope you aren't feeling any tension or anything between us. I'm glad we discussed this this morning."

She swallowed hard and held her gaze steady. "Me too. And I'm good. Thanks."

He waved as he turned toward the kitchen and headed that way. She watched him go. And the thump of her heart alarmed her. As he disappeared through the door, she spun toward the table and stared down all the drinks and tried to yank herself back to sanity. *She was not feeling what she'd just thought she'd felt. It was all her imagination.*

* * *

"Jace, come on in here and give me a hug." Josie Jane exclaimed the minute she saw him enter the kitchen and waved her hand at him. "Did you fellas enjoy seeing my Lila out there? Thanks for helping her out with the ice."

Jace went over and gave her a hug. Then he stood straight and looked down at her. "Yeah, she's ready to put drinks in ice, so we're going to grab it and get it in the tub for her. I know y'all are going to put on a good party tonight. You two have been putting on good parties for years and years."

"We try." Josie Jane beamed up at him.

"Yes we do," Ruby agreed, passing by on her way to the refrigerator.

He gave her a quick hug, too.

"At least everyone seems to like them, since y'all all keep coming back," Josie Jane continued. "When I get over this problem with my hip, I mean my back, we're going to plan some more gatherings. We are bored and it's time to get back to the way it used to be. I mean, if you fellas are interested in dancing parties and festivities like we did when y'all were all younger. No dangling off Ferris wheels, though."

Zack laughed as he lifted the lid on the freezer. "Oh wow, was that a hoot."

Jace grinned. "I remember that. Us fellas always had fun riding those rides. And sometimes getting in trouble."

Josie Jane slapped her thigh as she chuckled. "You boys did tend to push limits. But you're all grown up now and we figure you aren't going to swing out the side of your Ferris wheel seats and see who can climb down the fastest. Thank goodness that the one y'all did that on was a small one and not one of those gigantic things."

"I have to agree that me and Zack and his cousins and brothers were all a little off back then. Thinking something dangerous like that was a fun thing to do."

Zack laughed hard. "Well, thank goodness when you made it to the bottom, you hadn't broken anything and were still alive since you released a little sooner than you should have."

It was true. He had been clambering down the moving metal bars and, a bit too high, decided to let go and drop so he'd win. But it was too soon and he sprained both his ankles and spent four weeks sitting. "I don't do anything like that anymore. Sitting for that long with nothing to do drove me crazy until Gramps started picking me up and carrying me to the feed store every day. Not getting to ride my horses or help herd the cows was painful. Thank goodness I learned my lesson." And he had. He'd never taken a stupid risk like that again. He'd always been very thankful that sprained ankles had been all he'd suffered. But it had also been that he'd done a lot of sitting at his Gramps' feed store and Lila had spent a lot of time sitting there beside him. Making sure he wasn't lonesome. He pushed those thoughts away.

"Okay, we're going to carry the ice out and help get this show on the road. Lila's waiting on us." He crossed to the freezer and Zack did too. They lifted two bags each of ice and headed back into the main room. And there was Lila.

She'd taken the plastic wrappers from all the cases and stood ready to stick them in the ice bin. She looked really pretty in her red dress and sandals. Real good. Great…

He was going to have to try to focus not on how good or great she looked but how happy she was making her gram by being here. And definitely not on the fact that, at the moment, he felt kind of happy himself.

CHAPTER SIX

Zack finished pouring his ice into the ice chest and caught his buddy looking at Lila. His thoughts from earlier were right—Jace was still interested in Lila…maybe still in love. If the glimmer that he glimpsed in her eyes was correct, she, too, had lingering feelings for Jace. He'd always thought the way they'd broken up had been too bad. He hadn't been joking when he'd told Jace earlier that he needed to make her understand that what she'd thought happened wasn't the truth. He knew how it really felt when someone had an affair on you. And yeah, he'd never even considered taking that chance again. He'd loved once and been betrayed and wasn't having any more of it. Maybe that was the way Lila felt but she was wrong; unlike his situation, Jace loved her and would never have had an affair.

But he'd agreed to do what Jace suggested earlier, and they would both put themselves out there and dance with someone tonight. And he knew who he was dancing with. "Okay, is this enough ice?"

Jace finished spreading his out and looked from him to Lila. "We've got more in the freezer if you need it. We can go get it."

Lila smiled. She really was a beautiful woman, and her eyes shifted from him back to Jace. "I think it looks good. By the time I get all these drinks in there, the four bags should be enough." She reached for some of the cans and started pushing them into the tank. "Thank you both."

"I've got to do some things, but Jace, why don't you stay and help her? That's a lot of cans to put in this container and if she needs more ice, you can go grab it. It's been really nice seeing you, Lila. I think people are going to start arriving any minute now. It won't be long and this party is going to get started." He didn't wait for them to say anything, agreeing or protesting—he spun on his boots and headed for the back exit. He was on a mission.

His brothers and cousins had arrived and were setting hay bales out in the back area for people to relax on when they came outside to take a break and get fresh air. They were all dressed for the evening and lifting the bales off the back of the trucks and carrying them to their spots. Two bales forming the corner of a box scattered about the yard. It was something they'd always done and needed no one out here giving them instructions, so that meant no one but them were around and that was what he wanted.

He moved to the middle of all of them and waved his arms. "Hey, y'all come here. I've got something I need y'all to do tonight."

His brothers Ryder and Dustin were closest to him and stepped closer.

"What's up?" Dustin asked.

"Y'all come on, hurry." He waved the others to move closer.

His cousins, Ace and Hunter, plopped their bales down and strode over. His brothers Caleb and West reached him about the same time. Zack grinned at them, then glanced at the back entrance of the building, making sure Jace hadn't followed him. He hadn't and that was good. "Okay, guys, listen up, remember Jace and Lila, Miss Josie Jane's granddaughter, were engaged and planned to marry and then she broke it off and moved home?"

"Yeah, we remember," Hunter said and everyone else agreed.

"Okay, so here's the deal. She's finally, after all these years, back in town to help her gram. And me and Jace took the ice container in there and she's the one filling it with drinks. And me and Jace had already had a short conversation before we even went in and found her standing there. I'm telling y'all that Jace still loves her. Y'all know he's never dated but a few times then cut it out completely, like me...but I have real, true reasons. I think he needs to confront her finally with what she believed he did and that he didn't do. I don't know how in the world she could have believed it but that's not for me to understand. What I want is to give them a chance to at least talk about it. So, I've got a plan.

I promised him and he promised me before we went into the building that we would both stop standing on the sidelines like we always do and at least ask one lady to dance tonight. And so, I've now decided that I'm going to ask Lila to dance and was hoping each one of you would also ask her to dance."

Smiles instantly spread across the faces of his brothers and cousins, they got it. He chuckled. "Yep, I want to see what Jace's reaction is when she starts dancing all night long. I think if he's still as interested as I think he is, he'll get up and decide to step in and ask her to dance himself. And maybe we'll see a new romance break out. If not, then my guess is maybe he'll move forward and start dating again."

Ryder grinned. "I think it's a cool idea. I saw her and she's as pretty as ever. And I don't know, I'd kinda like to go for a dance with her." His grin widened.

Zack glared at his older brother, who made a game out of dating too many women. "Hey, no thinking of that. It's just a dance, okay? No trying to make a move, dude. She's off the market for any of us."

Ryder laughed. "I'm just teasing. She's always

been like a friend to all of us, and I'm glad she's back in town. I know her gram is thrilled. So I'm in. How about the rest of y'all?"

Caleb's wide smile took over his face and his green eyes danced—always in the mood for fun. "I'm in. Wouldn't miss it."

West joined in with his own grin. "I'm ready. I want to see what breaks out on Jace's face when all of us start dancing with what we've always considered his one true love. I think that was a huge misunderstanding and they need to work it out."

Hunter nodded. "I agree. I'm in too. Boy, this dance night has suddenly turned real interesting. Ace, what about you?"

The twins looked a lot alike but had distinctly different colored eyes. Hunter had blue-green and Ace had sky-blue eyes that danced as he grinned at them. "I'm all in. And I, like y'all, am hoping something good comes out of this. I mean, Jace, he doesn't hardly connect with anyone other than when he's at work. He dated a little while and then he got that big dog of his, and he spends hours out in that pasture, getting it the exercise it has to have. That's hiding out, if you ask me."

Everyone laughed, because it was true.

Dustin looked about the group. "The short time dating and the fact that he got a dog that needed extra exercise, thus time outside with the dog instead of out on a date was his plan…I think Zack is onto something. Let's do this."

Zack grinned at them all. "All right. Let's see what we can stir up, fellas." He raised his palm up and all his brothers and cousins slapped it. They were in, and he hoped it all came out good. If not, at least it might be a new beginning.

But in his heart of hearts, he hoped it led to a happy ending.

CHAPTER SEVEN

"Okay, Gram, here's your chair." Lila had carried a chair over and set it to the side of the food and drink tables, and also one for Ruby to sit at. They would have a wonderful time watching everyone and they'd have plenty of people coming by to talk to them. Red was still working but would be here soon, as would a lot of people. But there were a lot already arriving.

Gram and Ruby had been standing behind the food table, talking with some of the other ladies and they, too, might join them here with their chairs since she'd started the gathering spot with Gram and Ruby's chairs first. Her gram had seemed to be doing fine, standing up over there for the last thirty minutes, but she'd said nothing, letting her enjoy the moment. But now she needed to sit down, and Gram proved her to be right when she looked over at her with what looked like relief in her eyes.

"Thanks, darlin'. I was ready for that. That body exhaustion just sets in out of nowhere." She walked over and eased herself down into the chair. She looked up at Lila. "This is perfect. It's going to be a great evening. Just look at all the people coming in, smiles on their faces and visiting already. It's going to be fun."

"I think so too." Ruby sat down beside Gram. "I've always loved these things. And I tell you what, I'm anxious to see you out there dancing, Lila. It's been a long time, hasn't it?"

Lila swallowed hard. "Oh," she kind of laughed, "I don't think I'll be dancing. I'm just here for Gram, so I'll make sure the tables are supplied and if needed, I'll bring it from the kitchen. You two just sit there and enjoy yourselves as your friends come by and visit with y'all."

Both of them looked at her with disbelief. Gram was the first to speak. "I don't think so. You're going to dance. You're going to have fun. That's what you're here for."

"Your gram is right. It's going to be a fun night, and if you just stand over here with us, we're going to think that you are just here to take care of us. And believe me, we can take care of ourselves. We've been doing it for a long, long time."

She felt bad at their words. She hadn't meant to insult them, but by the looks on their faces she'd done exactly that. "Then…I guess if anyone asks me, I'll dance. At least with a few. I'm not dancing all night. Just so you know."

Gram and Ruby smiled at each other. "Sounds fine," Gram said, her voice tender. "I just want you to have fun. That music is going to get started here in a minute, and I'm going to enjoy watching you dance around for the first time in so very long. Too long. Maybe Jace will ask you to dance."

"No, don't go there, Gram. I don't think he'll be asking me, and I do not want you doing any kind of urging or suggesting or hinting to him. None of that."

Ruby crossed her arms and watched her. "Do you really think that for a young fella to ask you to dance, he's going to need encouragement?"

"I, um." *What had she done?* "Look, just don't push Jace, okay? It is complicated enough. And we've both agreed to ignore the past and get along for you, Gram. So we can have a good visit."

Gram sighed heavily, as did Ruby, but then nodded as they stared at her. Maybe they saw that she was stressed out at the pressure she was feeling. Jace had helped her finish putting the drinks in the ice and they had talked a bit about his cute dog. He'd said the dog was very busy and was probably home wishing he was out playing in the lake. She'd laughed, seeing him in her mind, that big dog loping like a horse through the edge of a pond or lake with a grin. She'd smiled and he'd laughed, and then they'd stared at each other for a few minutes. Then he'd said he needed to go help greet people at the front door and walked away. She'd been very, very relieved.

And now the party was starting. She moved behind the table, getting away from Gram and Ruby, hoping that the decision to be back behind them would help the two to remove her from their thoughts. As the band of older men, some she recognized from years ago, began playing music, Bo, Jace's granddad, stepped up to the microphone.

He tapped it. "Welcome to the town party. As usual, we are glad we've all gathered for this night of fun. It's good to celebrate living in a small town and having everyone want to gather together and party with you. So, here we go. Enjoy. And I hear there are lots of good desserts and appetizers back there and plenty of refreshments that everyone has brought. Kiddos, you can dance out here on the dance floor but don't run into couples or each other playing. And do not go outside without your parents. We want to keep an eye on you."

She remembered those same words back when she was younger and how all the kids had wished they could go outside and play chase in the moonlight and hide-and-seek in the dark but they weren't allowed. There was always that fear someone would get hurt and ruin the evening, so inside they'd remained. Things hadn't changed; everyone was obviously still very protective of all of them, wanting to keep them safe and that way, everyone would have a good time without having to worry. She understood it now, being an adult; she knew if she had a child, she'd want to keep them within eyesight too. But she had no child to worry about. The kids were over in the corner, already having a good time and not thinking about not getting to go out the back door. She, on the other hand, was and might sneak out the back and to a far corner in a bit to avoid some of the pressure she was feeling from her dear gram and Ruby.

The music was country, of course, because they were at a country dance. The singers—some locals— were good and could play the guitars and the piano. A few people came up and got drinks and plates of food, and she smiled and welcomed them. Though she didn't know any of them, she made sure she was friendly. She'd made sure the drinks were accessible and new ones were moved from the bottom to the top as the top one disappeared.

She just straightened up from being bent down, rearranging them, when Zack walked over. Lila smiled. "Hey, are you enjoying yourself?"

"I am and I decided—well, me and Jace agreed that we would both dance tonight at this dance since neither of us do anymore. I don't know how much I'm going to dance but I agreed to the challenge, and he did too so….since I watched you do all this work, I've come to ask you to dance. If you'll take a moment to relax out on the dance floor for a few minutes with me, then I'll have achieved my agreement."

Her insides trembled. She glanced at her gram, who was watching her. Gram grinned and so Lila only had one answer that she could give him. "Sure, I would love to dance with you. But I need to warn you that it's been a long time since I've been out on a dance floor."

He held his hand out to her, his eyes sparkling. "Don't you worry. I've been on the dance floor very little, too, so we'll just get out there and do what we can." He chuckled. "We'll make it through the song and both be able to mark on our chart that we danced at least one dance tonight."

She laughed at his words and humorous expression as she took his hand. "All right, perfect answer. Let's do this so we can say we did get out there and you came through on your challenge. Still, I am kind of shocked that you and Jace made that challenge between the two of you."

They'd reached the dance floor area, and he faced her as he held her one hand, then wrapped his free hand around and settled it between her shoulder blades. There was a comfortable space between their bodies, helping her nerves to relax.

He grinned at her. "Yeah, well, he and I both have kind of just been observers for the last several years." He took the first step and she followed his lead as they began the slow dance, with him leading the way. "I don't know if you realized this but after you left, Jace didn't date for a long time. And then he went out on a few dates and then he didn't. Me, I thought I found someone I was going to marry and then I saw, not an assumption but witnessed, her and another guy when I walked in on them. I wasn't happy and I haven't dated since then. Getting betrayed like that once was enough for me. But I'm just going to be upfront with you. What I experienced and what you think Jace did was two totally different things. I had direct sight of my fiancée's deception. You, on the other hand, have no proof of anything against Jace. I hope you've thought about that."

She stared at him, not really having thought he would be confronting her like this. "Did he get you to talk to me about this?"

He pulled away slightly. "Oh no, he has no idea I'm telling you this. It's just I'm curious about why you would believe that…well, that gal who has proved herself over the years not to be trustworthy. I mean, she's been married two times and all of her ex-husbands said she cheated on them with other people. Anyway—I'm sorry, I don't normally talk like this but I'm just asking why would you let someone like her break you and Jace up? Yes, all this has happened since you left town, but she had a reputation of being conniving to get her way even back then."

Her stomach felt sick. "I didn't have a view into the future of what she's done all these years in between. And what she told me seemed to be believable, from her point of view." Her insides rolled even more. "She said it was all true and cried telling me." The music was starting to wind down, and she looked around and saw people were watching them. She felt very vulnerable suddenly. "Look, I was young. And maybe I jumped to the wrong conclusions. But Jace didn't even try to change my mind. He never contacted me or followed me. I figured if he loved me, he would have tried to make me believe that she was wrong." *Why* was she telling him all of this? The music was coming to an end, and she was so glad. It was time to go find a hole to climb into.

"Well, maybe you were very convincing in getting him to believe that what you said was what you believed and always would. This is just my opinion but really, I'm glad you're home, so don't think me saying this is against that, but I'm going to be blunt. My good friend would never have done to you what my ex did to me. He's just not that kind of person. Then again, I bet it was a blow to him that you would believe he'd do something like that to you. I mean, if I was shocked that you would believe that about him then…have you ever thought about how shocked he was that the woman he loved would believe that about him?"

She blinked as he lowered his hand and released her. "I haven't thought about that."

"Well, I'm just pointing it out to you. Thanks for the dance. According to mine and his challenge this evening, I have now accomplished my part, so I can either ask someone else or I can go stand on the sidelines and watch everyone else. It's good to see you, and I'm glad you're back in town. Your gram is smiling right now, so that's a good thing."

He turned and walked away while she stood there, heart pounding and feeling light-headed, she took a deep breath and tried not to meet anyone's gazes as she headed off the dance floor.

* * *

"Hey, Jace." Ryder came up to where Jace stood near the back exit, watching the dance. "What do you think about your old girlfriend being back in town?"

Jace's gaze was glued to Lila and Zack dancing together. "I'm fine with it. Seeing her out there is good for her grandmother. She's missed her, and I've answered that question one too many times."

Ryder grinned. "I imagine you have. I figure there's speculation going on. So how do you feel about watching my brother and your buddy out there dancing?"

Jace gave him a "what are you doing" look, hoping to shut him down. "I'm not thinking anything about it. We haven't been together for years and now she's back in town. Me and Zack challenged each other to dance tonight since we've both been sidelining. So I guess he just decided he'd dance with Lila." *Like a good friend ought to*, Jace thought, feeling tension building. *He didn't care who went dancing with his ex-fiancée.* He didn't like the thoughts raging through his head, either.

Ryder grinned at him.

"Hey, don't be grinning."

"Whoa, I'm just observing. Maybe you need to go ask her to dance."

"No, I do not need to open that again."

"*That?* You mean being in love with someone and then just walking away?"

"Okay, okay. What is up with this?" he asked as out

of the sideview of his gaze Jace saw Lila headed back toward the concession stand are when West stepped up, smiled broadly and obviously asked her to dance too, because he waved his hand toward the dance floor. That expression crossed her face that he'd seen before, when she searched for the right answer—her gaze shot to the ground and then to her gram, who rolled her hand as if saying "go on, dance with him." Jace's gaze slammed back to Lila as she took a deep breath, gave a light smile and placed her hand in West's. Then they went back out onto the dance floor. Jace yanked his gaze off of them and found Ryder watching him, his smile gone.

"You going to tell me that look on your face has nothing to do with you caring that she's dancing with other men?"

"I'm going to tell you that you're my friend and I'm trying to figure out what you're trying to do, but I don't have to answer that question."

"I know. I was just asking. Anyway, I'm going to ask her to dance tonight, too, so don't be getting mad at me. If you don't care, then all roadblocks are gone. So, anyway, all you've got to do is say don't dance with her, and I'll back away."

After those crazy words, Ryder turned, and Jace watched him walk over to a group of cowboys standing closer to the dance floor. All of them were watching West and Lila dancing. *What was going on?* He glanced back out to watch them too, just in time to see West laugh as he engaged in a conversation with Lila. Lila who was now smiling. West's next words must have been funnier as she tilted her head back and laughed harder, her eyes sparkling.

Jace's gut knotted up and his chest yanked, as if he'd just been slammed with a hard fist.

This was not good.

He spun and marched out the rear door. He sucked in air, taking deep breaths as he stormed through the nestled hay bales all the way to the far back side of the yard. He stayed there, hidden away from everyone who had already begun to gather outside under the stars. There was romance going on, and couples who were married were out here enjoying the evening and atmosphere with each other and also conversations with friends. That's what a community gathering was all about. But he wasn't part of that right now; he needed space, thus here he was, at the edge of the fence line, staring out across the pasture that spread from this side of town. If he'd have had his horse, he'd have slung into the saddle and ridden away. Exactly what he'd done many times since she'd accused him of forsaking their vows of love all those years ago…

The fact that she'd believed that he would do that, have an affair on her—he yanked his hat from his head and ran his free hand through his hair. *How could she have even thought such a thing of him?* His temples throbbed; she'd been at least looking a little bit serious when Zack had been dancing with her. Then she'd looked like she was having a really good time with West.

He knew that it wasn't just Ryder who was watching him and trying to gauge what he was thinking. Others who had witnessed his pain were probably also watching to see his reactions from the sidelines. And he knew he had to suck it up and go back inside, or everyone would think he hadn't been able to watch her dance with other people. He didn't need that.

So, he took a deep breath, turned, and headed toward the back entrance.

He could do this.

CHAPTER EIGHT

"Hey there, Lila. I'm Genna Barry, and I own the dress store. Your gram has been so excited that you were coming to town. I've heard so many good things about you and I just wanted to come introduce myself and invite you to come over and see me at the store. I was going to come meet you at your grandmother's place, but I didn't have a chance today because between my online clothing store and the brick-and-mortar store, I could barely glance out the window much less come say hi." She chuckled. "Anyway, just wanted to come by while you weren't on the dance floor—I'm glad to see you really enjoying the dance."

"It's nice to meet you. I'd heard you had a great store, and I've seen some of your things and agree so

I'm coming in soon." She sighed. "So, you've noticed I'm on the ask-her-to dance list tonight. I think they all know it will make Gram smile and they are right so yes, I'm out there."

Genna chuckled. "You're making your gram happy and Ruby too. Two best-loved ladies in town. I think it's cool that you're doing it to make her beam like that. But…are you sure you're not doing any of it to make yourself smile?"

"I…well, I guess I did start enjoying it after I got out there on my second dance. West is funny and loosened me up. And Zack, well, he's funny too." He'd actually hit on a topic she'd not wanted to think about, but she didn't need anyone thinking he'd upset her. "Thank goodness they let me get away for just a little bit. And I need to thank you for preparing me for when I go over there, and Gram starts asking me questions." She chuckled. But it was true; it had been awkward, but she needed to let it go.

"That's great, and I have to say, West is a good one to make you smile," Genna said, her gaze moving from Lila to the group of men talking across the room, West one of them.

Interesting. "Oh, really? Does he make you smile?" *Why was she asking Genna that?* She had just seen a flash of attraction.

Genna's gaze locked with Lila's as a hint of pink flushed Genna's skin. "Aw, he's really nice but I'm not looking for love right now—I mean, I shouldn't have said love." She laughed nervously. "That's a little bit out there. Dating. I'm just not dating or looking for any kind of seriousness. So, no dating at all right now."

Well, well, well, that was interesting. "I understand completely. I haven't been open for that either. But did something happen in your past like it happened in mine?"

Genna waved her hand, then swept it through her long brunette hair. "Oh, I think everyone has a history. And I can say yes, I have a not-so-grand history also. But it brought me here last year and been meant to be. Your gram and Ruby and all the people here are really nice, so I opened my shop. And the ladies who have lived here all their lives really enjoy coming to the shop for new clothes. It was a great decision on my part."

"So what got you here in the first place? What's the story?"

"My mother, she's a roamer. She loves to travel and see the world. Yes, I come from a family that has the money to do that—to travel *all* the time. I traveled with her and my stepfather for years. My dad passed away right after I was born, and my stepdad is wonderful, and loves traveling as much as Mom. But for me, it got old. We traveled so much that I was homeschooled until I was able to enter college. I knew then that all that traveling for me was going to stop. I was finished traveling the world, so when I went to college and then my business and finally I started looking for a place to start my new life." She sighed and a big smile took over on her pretty face. "My mom had told me that she'd spent the summer here one time and that she'd enjoyed it. She'd been with her grandparents and stayed at a large ranch in a cabin because they were friends with the people. And, well, that stuck with me, and I decided to come see the town. I can tell you that when I stepped out of my car and looked down the street of this small town, something inside me clicked. I'd already opened my business online, so I could go wherever I chose. I decided to rent a house and stay a little while, and I met your gram and Ruby almost immediately at the diner after deciding all of that in the moment I was standing there, looking around. Those two are so happy here and helped me find a place to rent that day."

"Wow. That was a quick decision."

"Yes, but fantastic. I loved going to the diner every morning and visiting with everyone, your gram and Ruby and her husband Red—what a great man. And there were a lot of single cowboys everywhere. But I wasn't interested after what I'd been through in a disastrous college romance. At the end of my first week, when I was leaving the diner, I stopped in front of the empty shop next door, looked through the big glass window and decided then and there to open a real shop. I'd have a real clothing shop, not just my online shop. And I loved the idea of advertising that my shop was in this lovely little town. And believe it or not, people who love my online shop now set a goal to travel here just to come into my physical shop."

"Wow, that's wonderful and such a quick

decision."

Genna smiled. "*Yes*, but perfect! Everyone loves shopping in the real store, even my online customers. It's really been fun. I don't know if you've ever been to my website, but you'll see I have lots of pictures of clients who come from all over just to see the real store and the town. They buy things and we take our pictures together, one of the first customers' idea. Taking it with her, it hit me right then and I asked them if I could post it on my website. She said yes and it began. They *all* want to be on my website. I have fun, and it brings more customers here just to get their picture on the website. People have come to town who'd never before heard of the town of Lone Star, Texas—other than it being the second name for our Lone Star state."

"I always thought it was cool too. And this is a great story."

"I love it. And the customers I bring to town like going to the other stores and taking things home with them. Yes, this town called to me, and now I'm settled and call it home. But…back to dating. No, not interested. I had a terrible experience and am not going back there any time soon. Maybe never."

Lila found Genna interesting, and she understood her lack of desire to date again. "Well, I have to tell you that I think West is a really nice guy. And if you get to that point of wanting to date, if you give him a smile, he would probably ask you out. I can't really say that, but I just caught him looking at you while we were dancing and there was interest flickering in those stunning emerald eyes of his…so, just so *you* know, he is wonderful to dance with. Made me laugh and believe me, I needed to laugh."

Genna's gaze flashed back across the room, then back at Lila. "Nice, but a no for me. Not ready."

Lila understood and felt a bond with Genna, as if she had a friend. And it made her happy.

* * *

"So, you're just not going to do it." Zack leaned against the wall and studied Jace.

Jace frowned at his friend. "Okay, do what?" He was not in a good mood, and it must be obvious.

Zack looked out onto the dance floor, where his brother Dustin was now dancing with Lila. "You're not going to go ask her to dance?"

Jace stared across the room, watching Lila smiling at Dustin. Just like she'd smiled at Ryder, West, Zack, and their cousins Ace and Hunter. *All* of them had danced with her so far and it bothered him, as if his friends were just walking over and punching him in the stomach—and that *wham!* feeling bothered him. The fact that she could be gone all these years and come back and yes, draw this feeling of unsettled longing from him, hurt. And was driving him insane. He was exactly sure what it all meant but it didn't feel right.

It hit him then, and Jace glared at his good friend. "Zack, you did this on purpose, didn't you?"

Zack grinned. "Yes, I did. And it was because I wondered how you would react, and you answered my question. You're in denial, dude. You love that woman. You haven't given up what you felt for her. It's obvious, so my question is: are you not going to go fight for her?"

What? Jace looked around to make sure no one was within hearing of them. He'd been finding deserted spots to stand in all night, so thankfully no one heard their words. "Why would I want to put myself through that again? She believed something about me that she shouldn't have believed. I never did anything that I can think of that would make her think I would mess around on her. You know how much I loved her. And when she believed I would have an affair or even look at someone else—it was like she'd pushed me off a cliff. And man, I just couldn't climb back up it."

Zack uncrossed his arms and laid a hand on Jace's shoulder. "I know that's how you feel. It's obvious. Remember, I'm the one you talked to. And I'm the one who has been through something similar, except my love—not now but then she was—really did what you've been accused of. And yes, it's terrible that she thought that about you, but you don't know what that woman told her. You don't know anything behind the scenes because you didn't go after her and dig deeper. You didn't even try to get her to believe you." He dropped his arm and stared hard at him.

Jace glared at him, his insides rolling. They were buddies. They were the two guys who could always talk to each other. "Look, Zack, I know what you suffered, and I hurt for you because yes, yours was caught in the act, so no denying it. Unlike mine. And as much as I love her—I mean, loved her…" *Loved her…you know you love her still.* He shut that conversation in his head down. "But she didn't trust me. She walked away that quick and obviously never looked back. She didn't come back here because of me; she came back here to see her gram. And rightly so. Her gram has missed her so much."

He took a deep breath and not even on purpose, his gaze went out to the dance floor, where she was being held loosely in Dustin's arms. She smiled at him. *Oh, that beautiful smile.*

His heart clenched tightly.

He remembered holding her in his arms and how much it meant to him and how much he missed it. He'd dreamed about it and mourned the loss of her. Now, he wanted to walk across the distance between them and pull her from Dustin's arms and into his.

"Go ask her to dance. Just go," Zack urged. "This could be worked out. Dance with her and talk to her. She was young and obviously had been told big lies that she believed for some reason, and you didn't try to correct or find out why she believed the lies. I think she wouldn't have been so easily manipulated like that unless she had been scared to get married or been told some really terrible things."

The truth was, it could have been both. He was the one who so wanted to get married. He stiffened as that truth swept through him. She had wanted to wait, had worried they were rushing things. She'd assured him that she wanted to marry him, but he had wanted her then and wanted more between them. *Had he rushed her?*

The song ended and he stood there as still as a steel pole, watching. Dustin smiled at her, and she returned it then she headed back toward the refreshment area. She walked past the group that was now surrounding her gram. All the older women in town had pulled chairs up and some were knitting and others just smiling, talking and watching the dancing. It was like a gathering of a generation of ladies who had formed this town. They often gathered in the spot inside Josie Jane's Wash and

Repeat store like the older men in town gathered at the feed store, especially when his grandpa was working. Growing up, he and Lila had often hidden in the back of the stores and listened to the conversations between the ladies or the men. There was lots of laughter, and he and Lila had to work hard not to let their laughter rip wide and loud. He smiled now, remembering.

Now, as she'd smiled at her gram and her gram smiled at her, she continued to the tables she'd tried to stand behind all night. She'd stand there until another one of the fellas came and asked her to dance, and then she would once again go onto the dance floor. And he'd have to watch and wish…his heart raged as he stood there.

During the evening, she'd glanced his way a couple of times and his heart had stopped; then he'd forced himself to look away. But she'd beat him by a heartbeat and looked away first. Now her glance rammed into his, and he yanked his gaze away as he felt Zack's hand on his shoulder.

Zack pushed him slightly. "Go. Make this right. Or at least make it to where you can shut the door.

Watching you is hard. I mean, I'm no longer ready but I used to always want to be married before what happened to me happened and I slammed that door firmly. But I've been watching you, and in all honesty we don't either one of us want to be where we're at. Don't you remember when we used to talk about how we would each get married and raise our kids up as friends while we lived happily with our loves? Yeah, it sounds a little crazy now with the way our lives have turned out, but that's how we used to dream. And you know it. Now, we don't date; we stand in corners of dances alone and watch everyone else enjoying themselves. While they're all out there looking for love and we've slammed the door on it. Go. Get that door opened again, or closed between you and her so you can open it for someone else. But she deserves for you to try to make things right. Even though you didn't do anything wrong, take that step to get things right. The truth is that someone filled her with lies, broke her heart, and you never tried to fix it. Sorry, but that's the truth."

Jace stared at his friend as the truth rang through him. He hadn't ever tried to fix the lies. Yeah, he'd told her that night that what she was thinking was wrong but then he'd just shut it down, slammed the door, and she'd left. And that was the way it remained until she'd returned to town and Boulder had greeted her at the door, knocked her down and she'd looked at him with her beautiful, startled hazel-brown eyes as his sweet dog tried to lick her to death with his huge tongue.

His smart dog.

Jace yanked his gaze from Zack then headed straight toward the drink table.

He headed toward Lila.

* * *

"Lila, would you dance with me?"

Lila spun around at the sound of Jace's voice. She'd been putting fresh brownies out on a platter and now, startled, she was staring at Jace. "*Dance* with you?"

The question came out, the exact thing he'd asked her, but it was the only thing she could say. His words were stuck in her brain and her own words were going crazy, rumbling around, jumbled and incoherent to her.

He nodded, his gaze glued to hers. "Yes. I think, at least, it's a good place to start."

With the music playing and the pounding of her heart, she had a hard time hearing him. His gaze dug deep and looked…as if he were pleading with her? She had danced all night long with all his friends. It was as if they were trying to taunt him with her. She had laughed with some of the guys; they were all so nice. And yet despite everything telling her not to go there, her thoughts had kept going to Jace during every dance.

His best buddy, Zack, had planted thoughts in her brain when they were dancing. Then she'd seen Zack having a very intense conversation with Jace, and she had a feeling he'd done the same with Jace.

They had never talked.

He had told her he hadn't done what she'd been told he'd done. She'd been upset and had left town, and he hadn't come after her. "Yes. I'll dance with you." She'd said the words, and her heart thundered like crazy. Her stomach felt queasy with all the emotions suddenly raging through her. He took a step toward her and she almost told him no, that she'd been wrong to agree. But she didn't. When he held his hand out to her, she slipped hers into his.

Her gaze locked with his and his did the same as he took a step backward, tugging her to step with him, and then he turned and led her to the dance floor. Her heart pounded, as much as the room spun so she fought not to stumble because her nerves were fraying with each step they took. Everyone was watching them she could feel it. But more, she could feel her fingers tingling from his touch, just like they always had.

They reached the dance area and he turned toward her, lifted the hand he held so that hers rested against his heart and he wrapped his free arm around her waist. Her heartbeat heightened when they began moving with the music. She rested her free hand on his arm, her fingers tingled with the want to wrap around the back of his neck and gently play with the dark waves of hair. They had always danced that way, but she restrained the want to do it now. Thankfully he hadn't pulled her as close to him as he used to; he'd left a space between their bodies—a small gap. Still, she could feel every ounce of him radiating to her, through her as his deep-brown dazzling eyes held hers, just like he'd once held her heart.

The song played—a country song but her mind was reeling and she couldn't even come up with the name— as they moved slowly, so smoothly to the tune she couldn't look away from him, and her world spun in the depths of his gaze.

Then she felt his thumb on the hand holding hers against her back as it traced along her thumb, sending jolts of lightning through her, just like it had all those years ago.

"I should have followed you," he said, faintly but firmly. "I should have tried again to make you believe that I hadn't done what you thought I did—because I hadn't done what she accused me of. Do you think…" His words died and his gaze flickered, then he looked past her.

Lila's heart seized and she longed for his gaze to come back to hers. "I didn't give you a chance." It was so true. She felt so horrible. *Was it just the fact that he was holding her and she had grieved the loss of his touch for so long?* She'd believed he'd done something so horrible to her, to their love, but now, as his eyes found hers again, she faced what had plagued her until she'd shoved it in a dark closet of her heart. "I think maybe my uncertainty on whether we should get married so soon or wait might have played a part in my running. I actually am so sorry that I believed such things about you. In truth, I might have done you wrong instead of you doing me wrong." The truth slammed into her and she stumbled.

He held her, shifting so their bodies touched lightly as his eyes grew sad. "You weren't ready to get married, and you expressed that to me. I wanted you so badly that I didn't listen to you. Your worries were that we were rushing things. Rushing things because you weren't ready to take the next step in the relationship and, well, I was. You wanted marriage before we took that deep step into intimacy. I'm sorry. I let my want of you to lead my decisions. My decisions. My wants—not yours."

His words penetrated deep, drowning out the sound of the music and the anguish she'd felt.

"I, I don't think now is the time to talk about this."

Her heart pounded even more than it already had been. She needed space; she needed off the dance floor. She could feel the eyes of everyone watching them. "This is private, and I don't know if you realize it but everyone is watching us."

"Oh yeah, I realize it. But I had to ask you."

The song was coming to the end and she was relieved. She stepped back, giving them a little bit of space. "I think I'm done for the evening."

"I'm not going to bug you. But can we talk again? Can we finish or continue this conversation?"

She breathed in and nodded. "Yes." And then, before she said anything else, she spun away and strode off the dance floor, and bypassed Gram, who she could feel watching her. Bypassed the refreshment table and walked into the kitchen then out the side door there instead of the one that led into the back area. She inhaled deeply as she strode to the car right next to the door, her gram's, she yanked the door open and slid into the driver's seat. She gripped the steering wheel with her trembling fingers, then dropped her forehead to her knuckles. She breathed in and out, trying to calm the trembles that were not going away.

The door on the passenger side opened. She looked over as Gram slid into the seat.

"Can you drive us home?"

Lila sat up straight and let out a sigh of relief. "Yes, Gram, I can."

"Then drive sweet girl."

And she did.

They arrived home just a few moments later. They hadn't spoken again, though her gram did reach out and gently rub her arm as she continued to grip the steering wheel with both hands. Finally she drove the car into the carport, cut the engine off and they both climbed out. Her gaze flew to her red jeep and she almost dove at it in the need to get away. But she didn't.

Gram walked to the front of the car and waited for her.

"Are you okay? Steady enough to get inside by yourself?" she asked her gram, not planning to go inside just yet. But despite the stress weighing on her, she had to protect Gram.

"Actually, I'm doing great." Gram held her gaze.

"Are *you* okay? I was so glad to see you and Jace finally head out onto that dance floor. But, I could tell when the song ended that you were hurting." Her voice shook with emotion.

"I'll be fine." Somehow, someway, she would manage.

Gram looked as if she were going to cry. "I have to be honest. I brought you here under exaggerated circumstances. Yes, I hurt my lower back but it's not hurting as bad as I've pretended. I've just missed you deeply, and I had you on my mind so long. And I kept thinking that if I could get you back here so you saw that sweet man—because he is sweet. That young man and many others in town, but especially Jace since he's right next door to the store, make sure that I'm okay in my shop each day. If I need anything heavy moved in or out, he's the first one there because he's usually the first to see it. If he doesn't, his granddad Bo does and pulls him from the back to come help, which is good because I don't want Bo hurting his back any more than it already is after all the heavy things he's carried in that feed store. Jace always comes immediately and helps me.

He's a wonderful guy…and, his granddad and I talked."

Gram fiddled with the edge of her shirt and Lila waited knowing something was coming.

"Lila, neither one us believed Jace did what you thought he did. So, I did this, pretended I was hurt worse and you instantly came to help me." Her expression was as distressed as her voice. "To be honest, I missed you so much. But I hope, pray, that you'll forgive me and maybe some good will come from you coming home."

Lila couldn't move. Her heart had been aching but now, realizing her gram had been pretending to be hurt worse than she was just to get her back here…to give her a chance to straighten this out, slammed into her. She could have been furious. She could have blown up and stormed into the house, pack her things and then drive away. Leave everything that had happened behind…Just like she had done the first time.

Instead, she stepped forward, tears filling her eyes as she wrapped her arms around her dear, sweet gram. "Thank you. Yes, I know what you've done is a twist on the truth, but I needed to come back. Now, I've got to think. I've got to get my mind straight…and my emotions."

She pulled back and smiled at her gram, who was wiping tears from her eyes.

"You take all the time you need. And if I can do anything, please let me know," Gram said gently, then walked to the door, entered it, and closed it behind her.

Lila stood there, then followed the stone path that led around the edge of the house to the back porch. She sank down into the cushioned chair with the moonlight glowing down on her. She took a deep breath and let her thoughts begin to explore what she needed and wanted to do.

* * *

It was Sunday morning and Jace had sat out on the back porch until late the night before after he'd left the dance. He'd stood there on the dance floor and watched Lila walk out of the building, and watched her gram follow her. Unable to think straight he'd headed for the front entrance and strode down the sidewalk to his truck. But he'd sat there and waited until she drove from the side parking lot and headed down the road.

Life was complicated.

Now, sitting in the saddle of his horse, he followed Boulder as the animal raced—of course—toward the lake that held memories and regrets. But this morning, as much as he didn't want to go there, as much as he didn't want to think that she was going to walk away from him again, he followed his dog. Even if she understood what she'd put him through and wanted to give him another chance…everything was a blur.

He should have worked harder to prove to her that he hadn't and wouldn't have done what she believed. But that wasn't the whole case; he knew it now. He had rushed her. He had pushed her to marry him quickly and for all the wrong reasons. He'd loved her desperately—still loved her, and he knew it. But she moved slower than he did, and because he'd pressed her, she had conceded. But then everything that happened had been too much. And until last night, he had never let the part of rushing her filter into his thoughts.

Yes, they had loved each other, and they had both messed up.

He watched as Boulder raced up the hill and disappeared over the ridge leading to the lake. He followed just a bit behind the dog; he hadn't quite reached the top of the hill when he heard a scream that ended in a huge splash. And then laughter and gurgles erupted.

"Yah," he yelled, urging his horse forward. They topped the hill and there in the water was Boulder, standing on top of Lila. She was lying in the lake, her shoulders and head sticking up as the dog stood— probably on her hips. She had grasped him around the neck as the dog licked her on the side of her face once again.

He galloped his horse down the ridge and into the water and slid out of the saddle and landed in the water next to them. He grabbed the wiggling, clearly happy dog by the collar and tugged him off the laughing, grinning Lila. Her eyes locked with his as he tugged the dog away from her.

"I'm so sorry. Are you okay?"

Her voice rumbled with laughter. "I think I am. I was being knocked down, licked, and rescued at the same time by this wonderful large dog of yours."

Boulder struggled to get to her again, and Jace held him tight as the overly friendly animal lapped his long tongue from one side of his mouth to the other. Jace shifted between Boulder and Lila, and with his free hand, he grasped her just under her bicep and helped as she stood up. She wobbled and laughed as she got steady; then she leaned forward and cupped the grinning dog's face between her palms. Boulder wiggled all the more, lapping that tongue from side to side as she laughed.

She looked up at Jace, her eyes still shinning. "I couldn't sleep, so I came here about thirty minutes ago. I told Gram I wouldn't be going to church this morning but that I'd be with her next week. But I couldn't today. I needed to think, Jace." She let go of the dog and scanned the lake that had been their favorite spot, and then she looked back at him.

He couldn't speak. He could only stand there, his heart pounding as he wanted to reach out and pull her into his arms. Instead, he held his dog away from her—his dog, who had gotten to kiss her. He so longed to do it himself. Maybe not lick her face down like that but take those beautiful lips of hers with his and make the long-ago memory of kissing her back to a reality.

Finally he asked, "How's your thought process going?"

She pulled her eyes from his and walked the short distance to the bank.

He followed; then, at the shoreline, he looked down at Boulder. "Sit," he demanded in a firm, no-nonsense tone. The dog sat. "Stay." Again he said the word firmly, and he knew this wonderful but excitable animal would mind him, because one thing Boulder knew was that, when he heard that demanding tone in Jace's voice, he meant what he said. And right now, he needed his pup to behave.

Boulder flopped his short tail and basically gave him a smile as he cocked his head to one side and let his long tongue slide out, in his way of grinning.

Oh, if only Jace could feel that joy he saw in his dog's eyes. This dog that had given him comfort and help through these years of loss and separation he'd been living. He tore his gaze away from Boulder and met Lila's gaze. She'd been watching him with intensity and now she wrapped her arms together, as if holding herself up.

"Jace, I reacted too quickly. I wanted to marry you so badly and yet I wasn't quite ready to make that commitment. I had barely started college, and I was torn between you and school. I just didn't let myself think about why I so quickly believed that woman and not you. I apologize. I'm so sorry. And if I hurt you, I really, deeply apologize for that."

"I have the same apology to make to you. I wanted you so much. I wanted you in my life as my wife, as a man who loved you and wanted you. But I rushed you. And all of that aside, I should have followed you and we should have had this conversation."

"If it helps you feel better, I don't think I was ready for this conversation then. I think, because I wasn't quite ready to make a lifelong commitment, despite loving you so deeply, I think that rumor that woman started was just an excuse for me to run. And it feels so horrible right now."

His heart pounded. *Was there a chance?* "So, is

there a possibility we could start over?" Unable to stop himself, he took a step toward her. His hands were clutched tightly into fists to keep them from expanding and reaching for her. His heart was ready to explode. And then she stepped toward him and a gentle smile trembled on her beautiful lips and those pretty, hazel eyes danced in the rising sun like sparkles of gold.

"Well, I'm not so sure about starting over. How about… Oh Jace, I love you. I never stopped loving you. And my gram, such a smart woman—and your granddaddy, too—they were sweetly conning together to get us to this point. I'll have to tell you all the details later but I just don't have time at the moment because I have much more important things on my mind. Jace, I love you and if you'll have me, I'll marry you this minute."

He didn't say anything; he scooped her into his arms and lowered his lips to hers. Years of aloneness— of loneliness, of trying to zero out thoughts of how wonderful it felt to kiss this breathtaking woman—this woman who was beautiful inside and out—melted away. He spun them and kissed her, and she clung to him. Nothing had ever felt so perfect.

As they'd spun, they were now standing in the water and he shifted her up so that she was now higher than him, his head was leaned back as she kissed him. She was kissing him.

Now, she moved her lips from his and cupped his face and looked into his eyes. "I love you so much. And that—" She laughed as she looked down past him, and he realized that Boulder had come up beside them. He gave a bark and rose up on his hind legs and plopped his front feet on Jace's shoulder so he was now almost eye to eye with beautiful Lila.

"I can't blame him for wanting to get close to you but please don't kiss him. Just kiss me again and we'll marry as soon as we can get that license. *And* I can tell you this whole town and all of my buddies are going to be so happy. You do know that they were all dancing with you—yes, you are beautiful and wonderful—but they knew that this was where we belonged and they were taunting me so that I'd step out and make things right."

That beautiful smile spread wide. "I figured that

out. And I'll always be grateful to all of those Buckleys, they are awesome wonderful men." And then she dropped her lips to his and the kissing began again. But this time, it would go on forever.

And then Boulder got so excited, he yelped and jumped hard against them. They all fell into the water, rolling about and laughing all the way as the bells on Boulder's collar jingled and their spirits and hearts merged together with what the future held for them.

More Books by Hope Moore

Billionaire Cowboys of Lone Star, Texas

Sweet Love'n Cowboy

Heart Love'n Cowboy

Love Catch'n Cowboy

Happy Dance'n Cowboy

Real Love'n Cowboy

Forever Love'n Cowboy

McCoy Billionaire Brothers

Her Billionaire Cowboy's Fake Marriage

Her Billionaire Cowboy's Fake Wedding Fiasco

Her Billionaire Cowboy's Trouble in Paradise

Her Billionaire Cowboy's Secret Baby Surprise

Her Billionaire Cowboy's Second Chance Romance

Her Billionaire Cowboy Fake Fiancé

Her Billionaire Cowboy's Inconvenient Marriage Blessing

Billionaire Cowboys of True Love, Texas

Billionaire Cowboy's Runaway Bride

Billionaire Cowboy's Wedding Crasher

Her Billionaire Cowboy's Hill Country Proposal

Billionaire Cowboy Auctioned at Christmas

Billionaire Cowboy's Dream Come True

About the Author

Hope Moore is the pen name of an award-winning author who lives deep in the heart of Texas surrounded by Christian cowboys who give her inspiration for all of her inspirational sweet romances. She loves writing clean & wholesome, swoon worthy romances for all of her fans to enjoy and share with everyone. Her heartwarming, feel good romances are full of humor and heart, and gorgeous cowboys and heroes to love. And the spunky women they fall in love with and live happily-ever-after.

When she isn't writing, she's trying very hard not to cook, since she could live on peanut butter sandwiches, shredded wheat, coffee...and cheesecake why should she cook? She loves writing though and creating new stories is her passion. Though she does love shoes, she's admitted she has an addiction and tries really hard to stay out of shoe stores. She, however, is not addicted to social media and chooses to write instead of surf FB - but she LOVES her readers so she's working on a free novella just for you and if you sign up for her newsletter she will send it to you as soon as its ready! You'll also receive snippets of her adventures, along with special deals, sneak peaks of soon-to-be released books and of course any sales she might be having.

She promises she will not spam you, she hates to be spammed also, so she wouldn't dare do that to people she's crazy about (that means YOU). You can unsubscribe at any time.

Sign up for my newsletter here!

I can't wait to hear from you.

Hope Moore~
Always hoping for more love, laughter and reading for you every day of your life!

www.ingramcontent.com/pod-product-compliance
Lightning Source LLC
Chambersburg PA
CBHW070658100726
47907CB00007B/2251